D0914745

WATER PIRATES FROM OUTER SPACE

BY DAVID ORME

STONE ARCH BOOKS
www.stonearchbooks.com

Library of Congress Cataloging-in-Publication Data
Orme, David, 1948 Mar. 1–
  [Boffin Boy and the Invaders from Space]
  Water Pirates from Outer Space / by David Orme; illustrated by Peter Richardson.
  p. cm. — (Billy Blaster)
  Originally published: Boffin Boy and the Invaders from Space. Watlington:
Ransom, 2007.
  ISBN 978-1-4342-1267-2 (library binding)
  1. Graphic novels. [1. Graphic novels. 2. Heroes—Fiction. 3. Science fiction.]
I. Richardson, Peter, 1965– ill. II. Title.
PZ7.7.O76Wat 2009
741.5'941—dc22   2008031348

Summary:
Earth's oceans and lakes are starting to shrink. Billy Blaster follows the missing water as it
is sucked up into outer space. It looks as if the water is being stolen by an alien army. Will
Billy be able to stop these thirsty space lizards before all of Earth is turned into a desert?

Creative Director: Heather Kindseth
Graphic Designer: Carla Zetina-Yglesias

1 2 3 4 5 6 14 13 12 11 10 09

Printed in the United States of America

BILLY BLASTER

written by
DAVID ORME

illustrated by
PETER RICHARDSON

WATER PIRATES FROM OUTER SPACE

Alien space ships are on a mission.

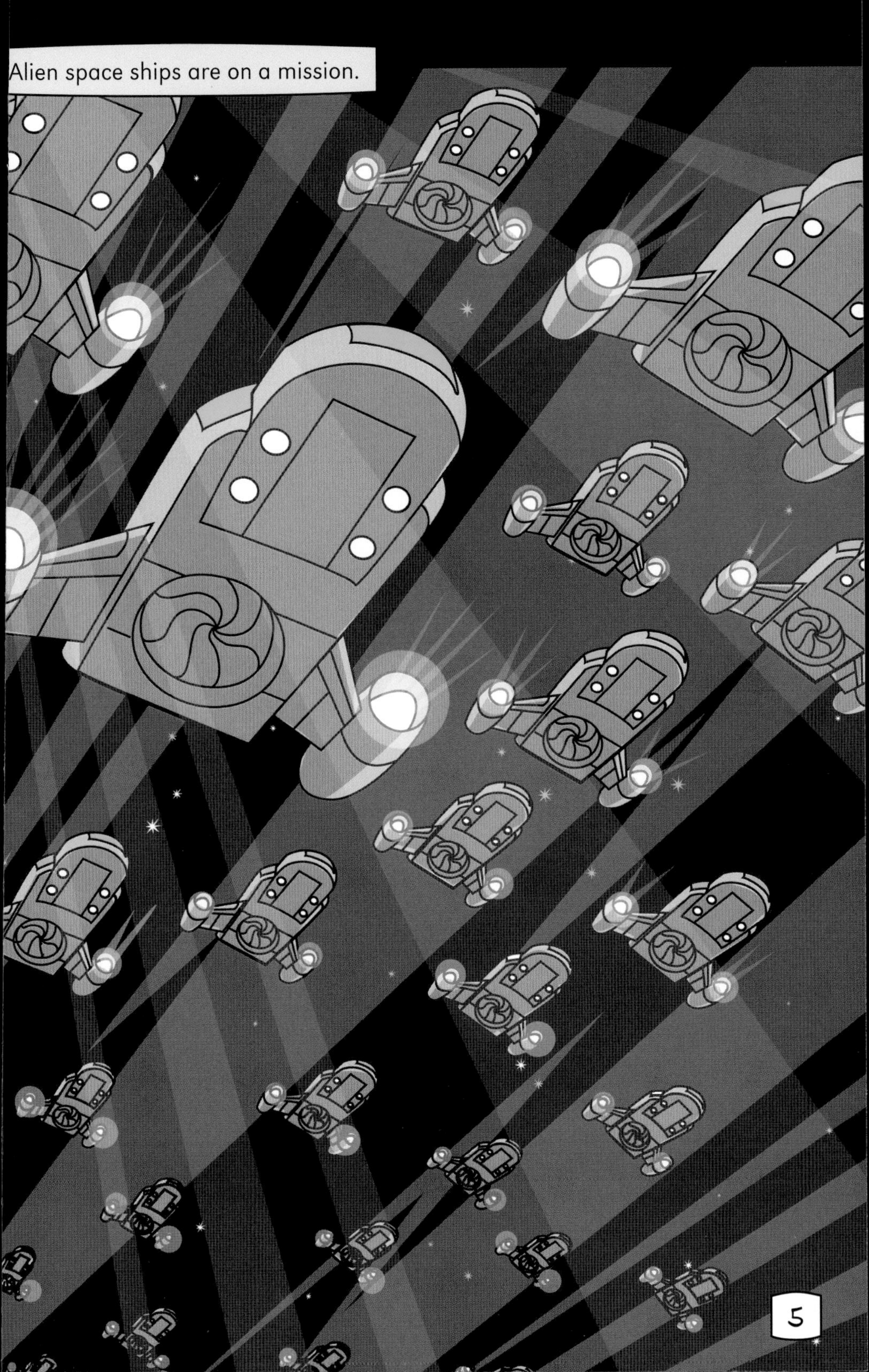

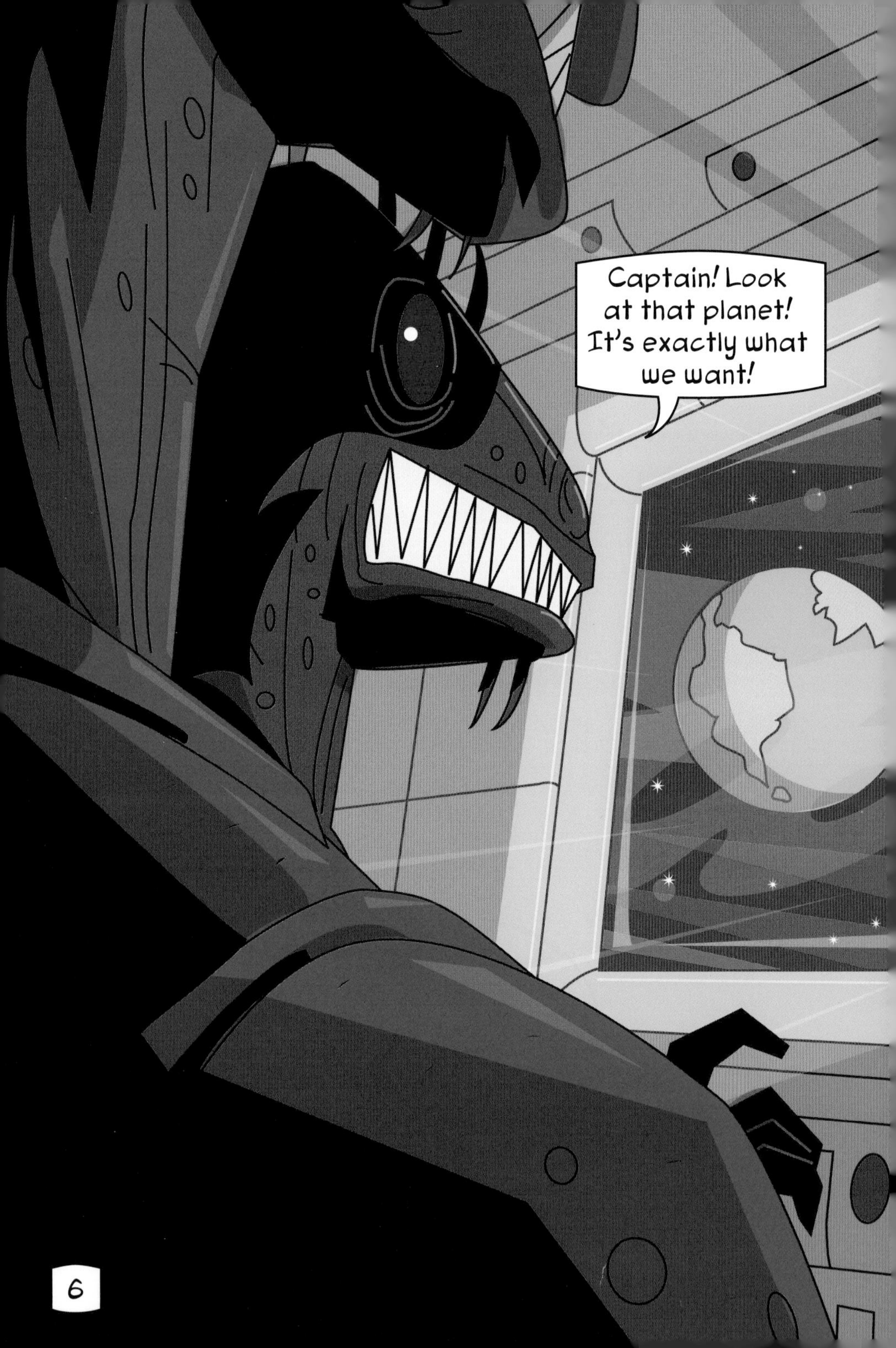
Captain! Look at that planet! It's exactly what we want!

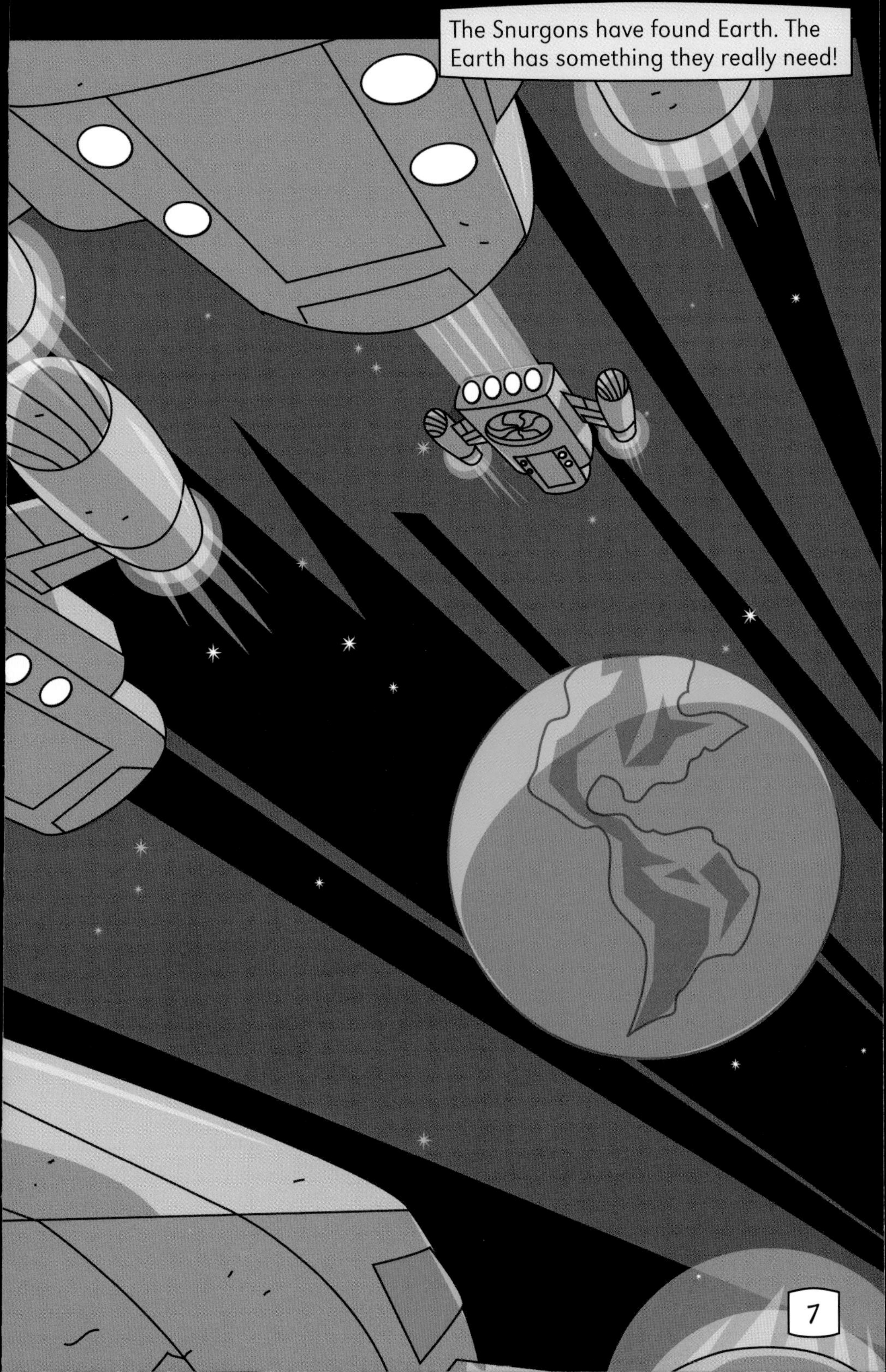
The Snurgons have found Earth. The Earth has something they really need!

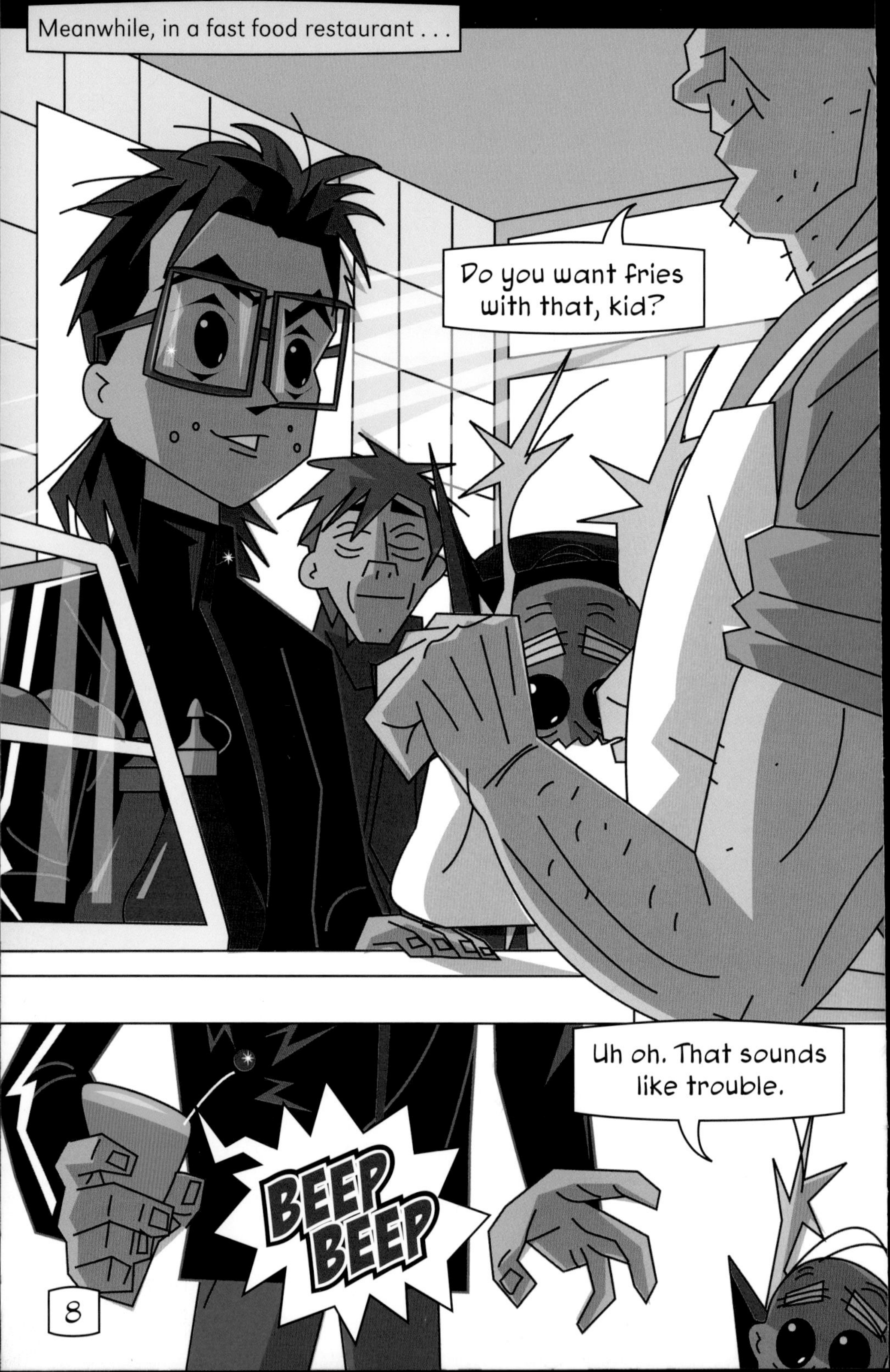

Meanwhile, in a fast food restaurant . . .
Do you want fries with that, kid?
BEEP BEEP
Uh oh. That sounds like trouble.

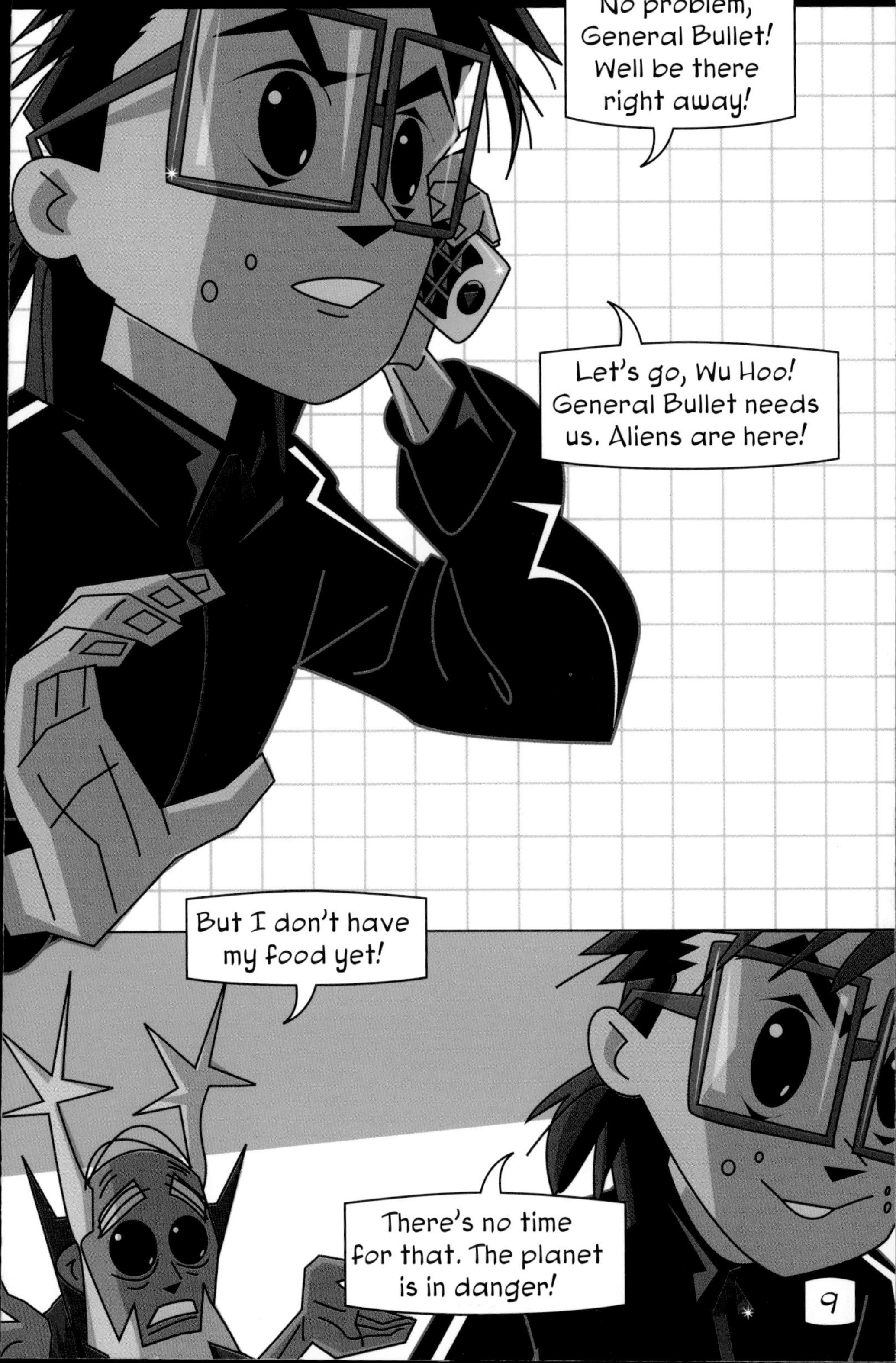
No problem, General Bullet! Well be there right away!
Let's go, Wu Hoo! General Bullet needs us. Aliens are here!
But I don't have my food yet!
There's no time for that. The planet is in danger!

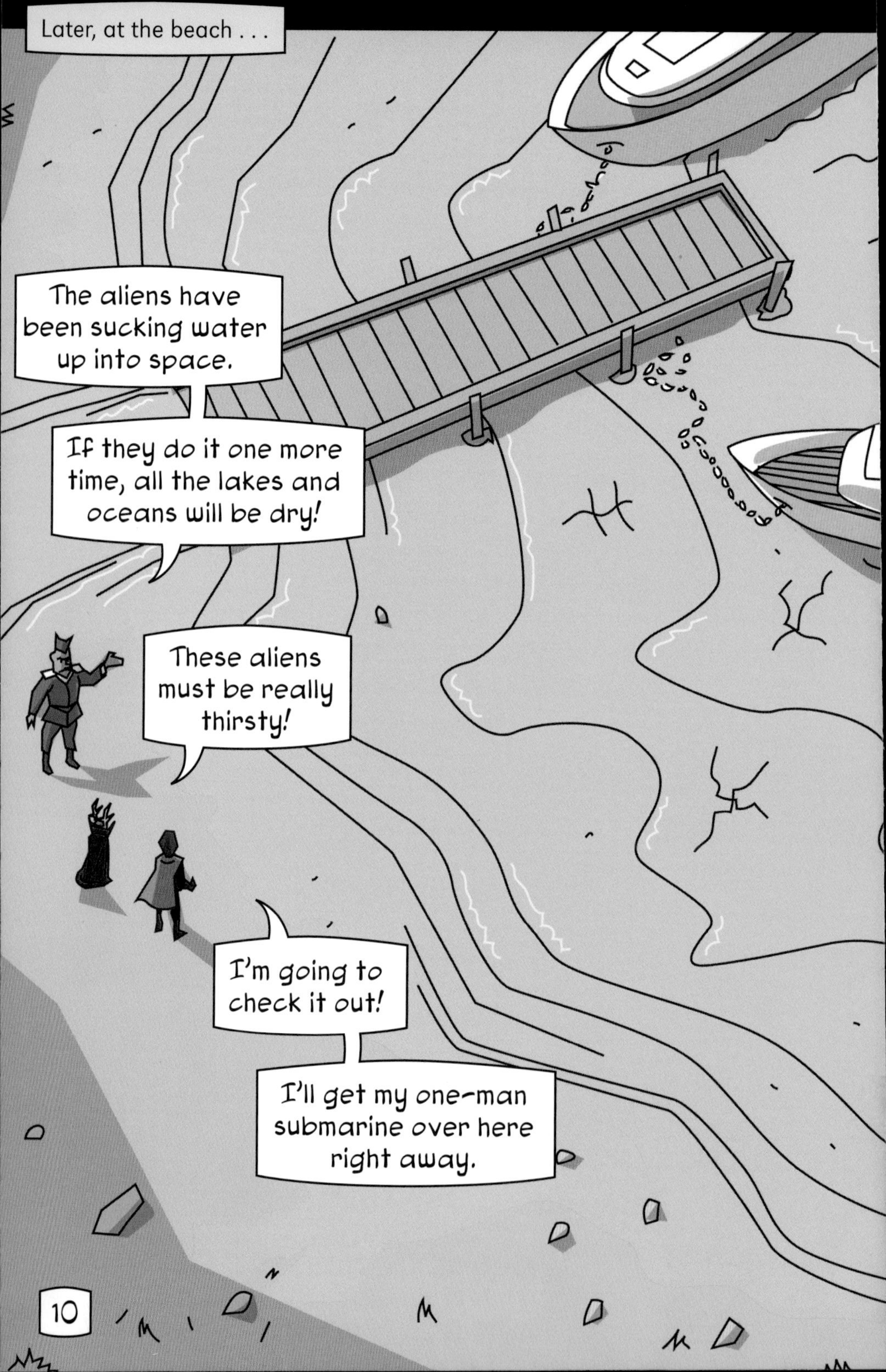
Later, at the beach . . .
The aliens have been sucking water up into space.
If they do it one more time, all the lakes and oceans will be dry!
These aliens must be really thirsty!
I'm going to check it out!
I'll get my one-man submarine over here right away.

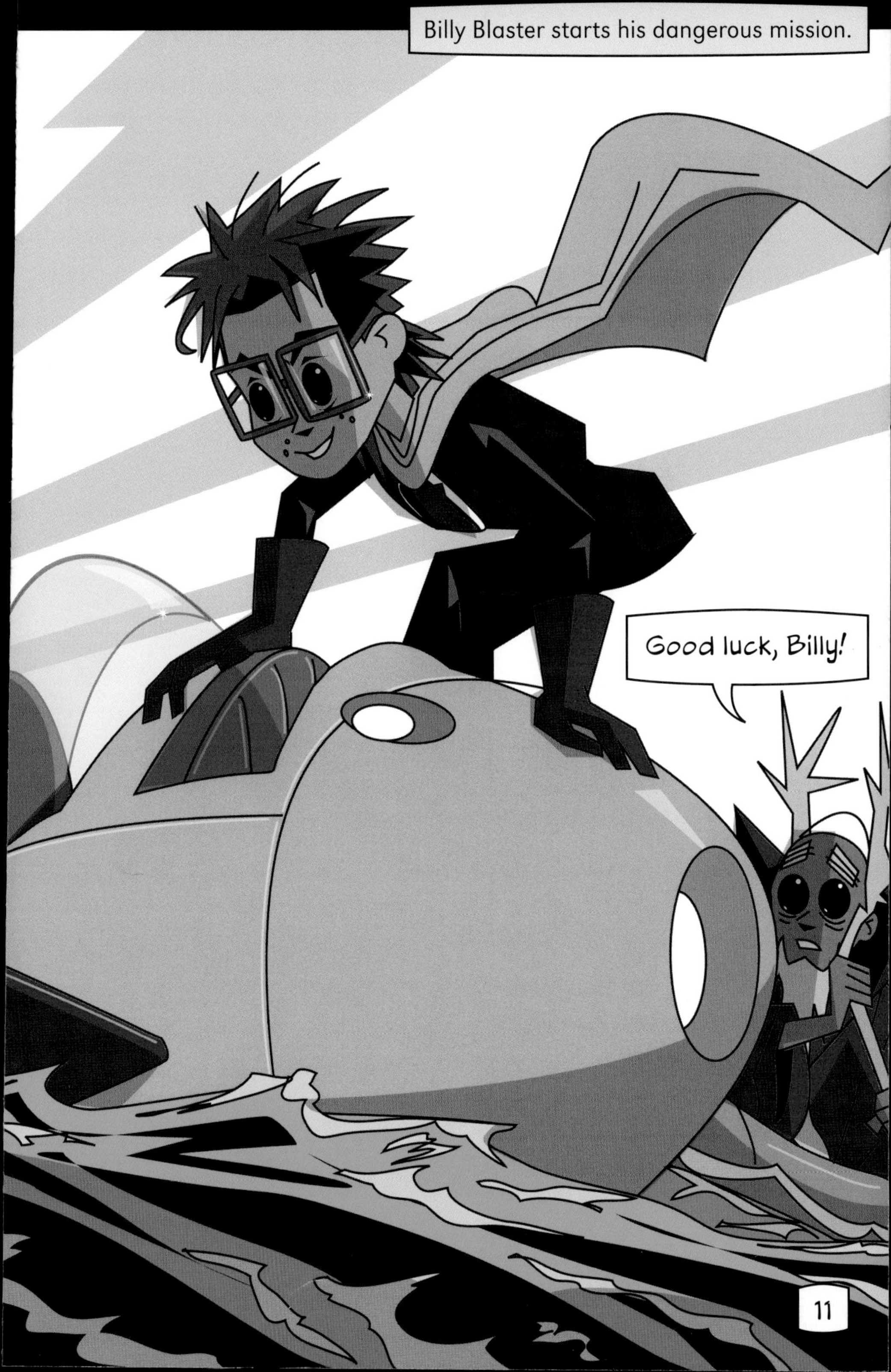
Billy Blaster starts his dangerous mission.
Good luck, Billy!

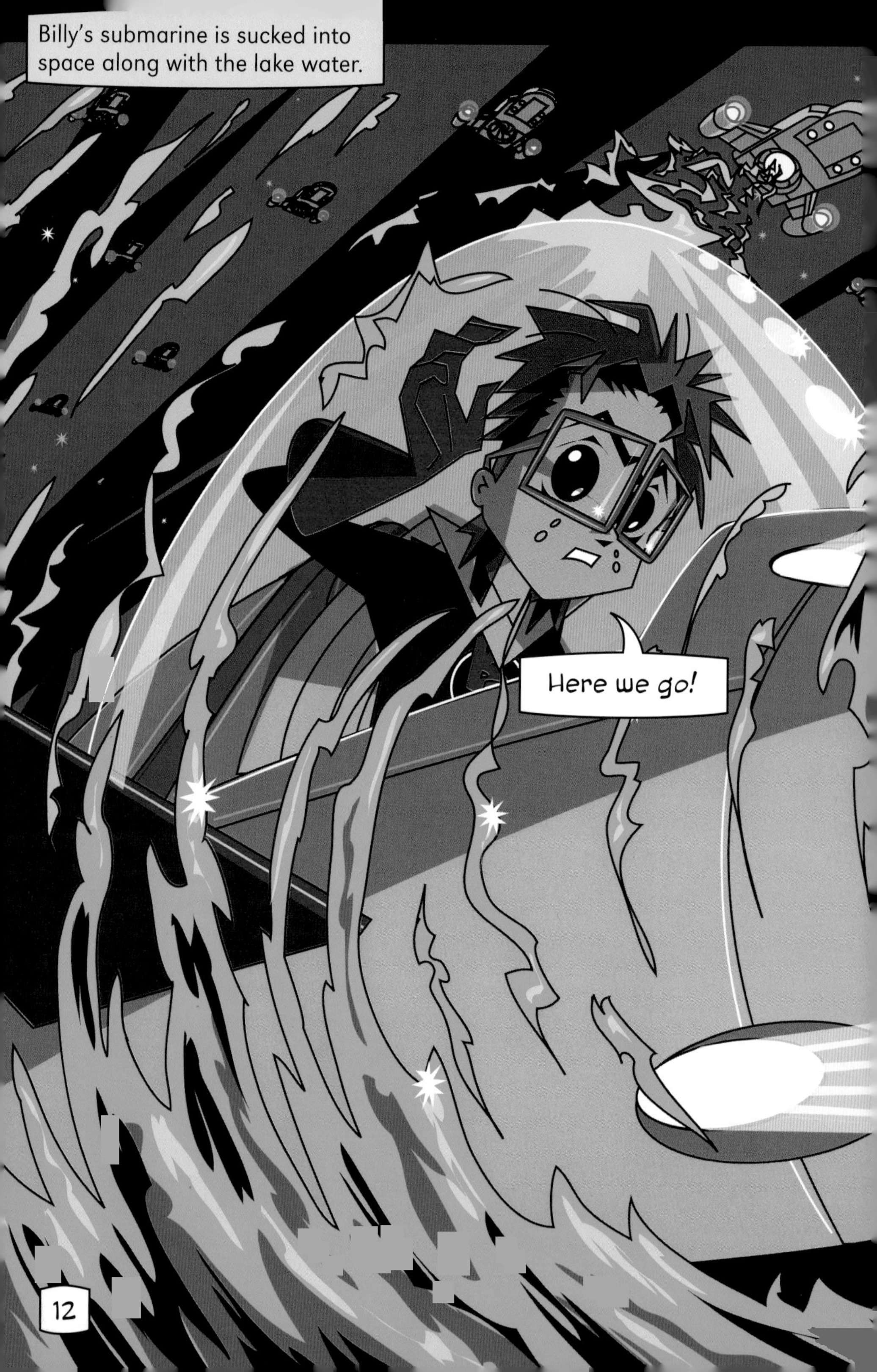

Billy's submarine is sucked into space along with the lake water.
Here we go!

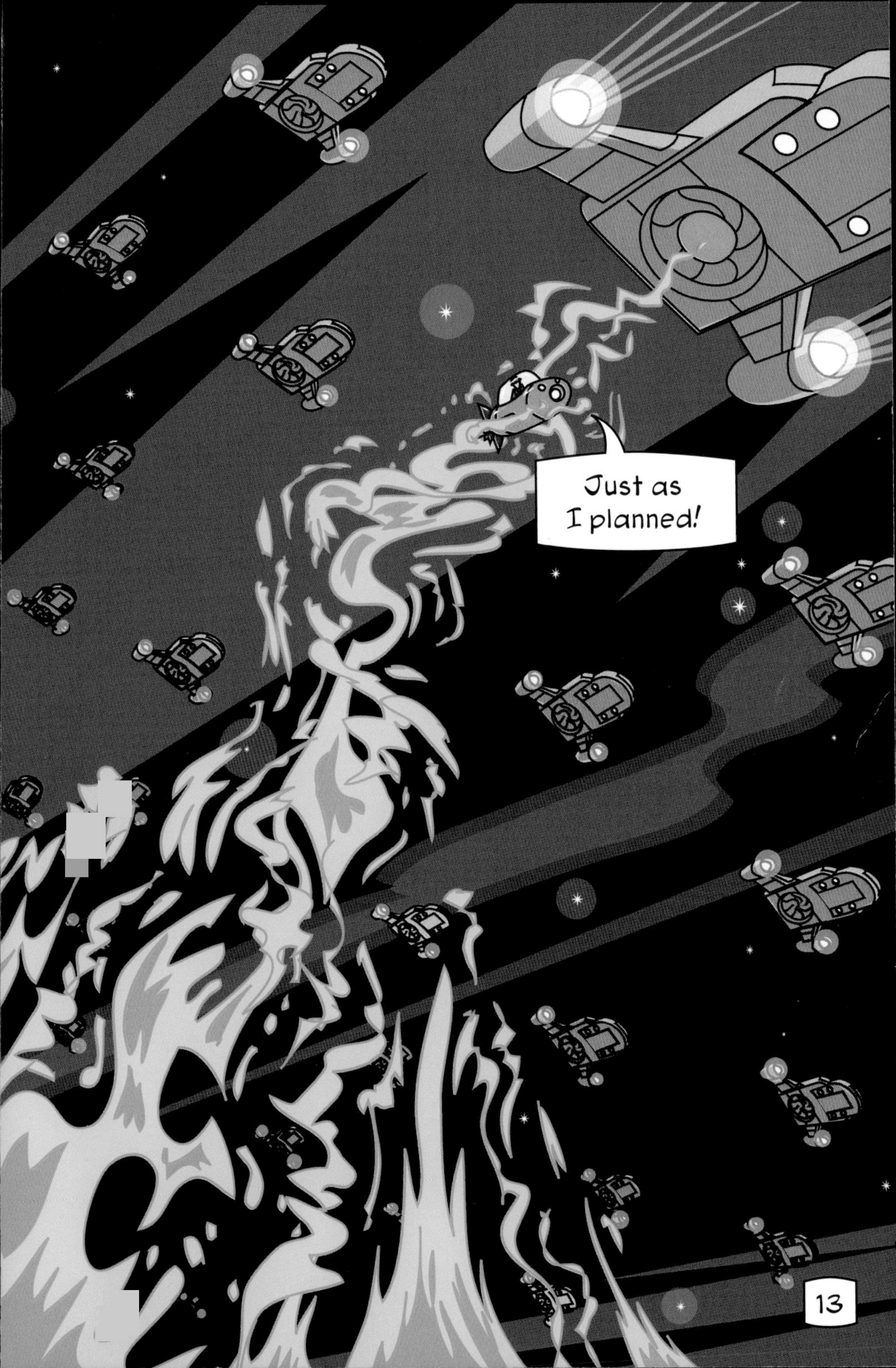
Just as
I planned!

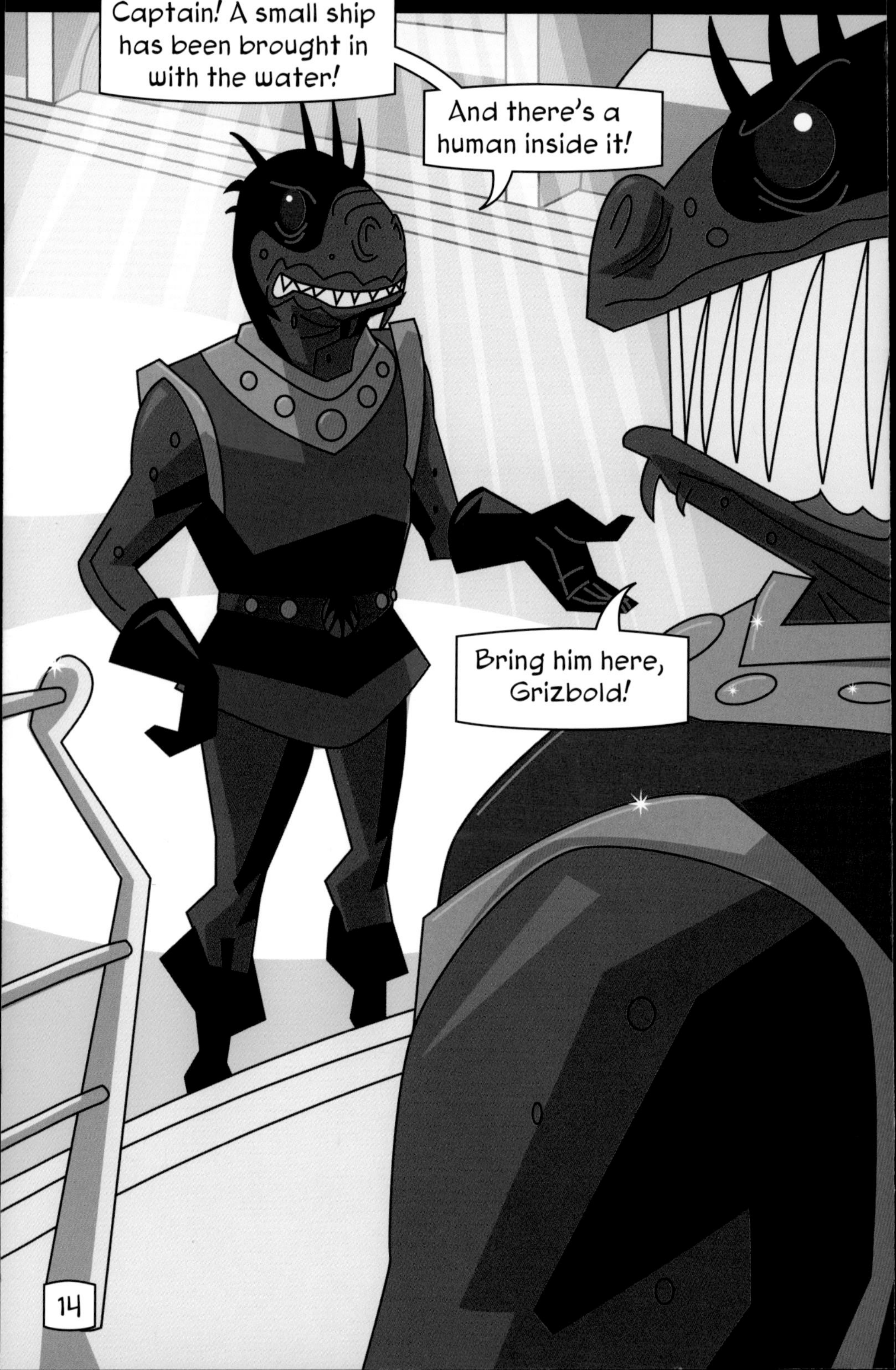
Captain! A small ship has been brought in with the water!
And there's a human inside it!
Bring him here, Grizbold!

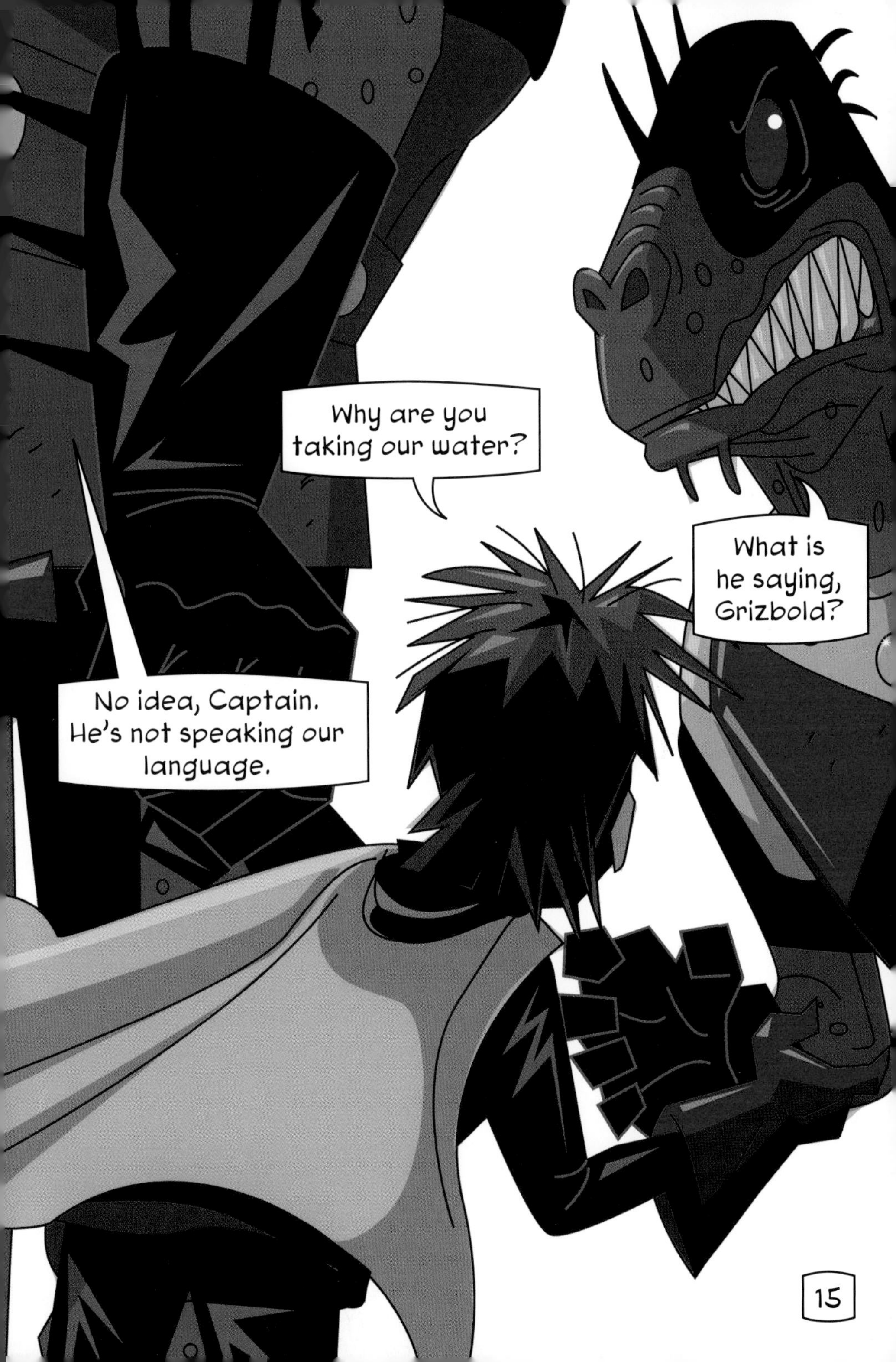
Why are you taking our water?
What is he saying, Grizbold?
No idea, Captain. He's not speaking our language.

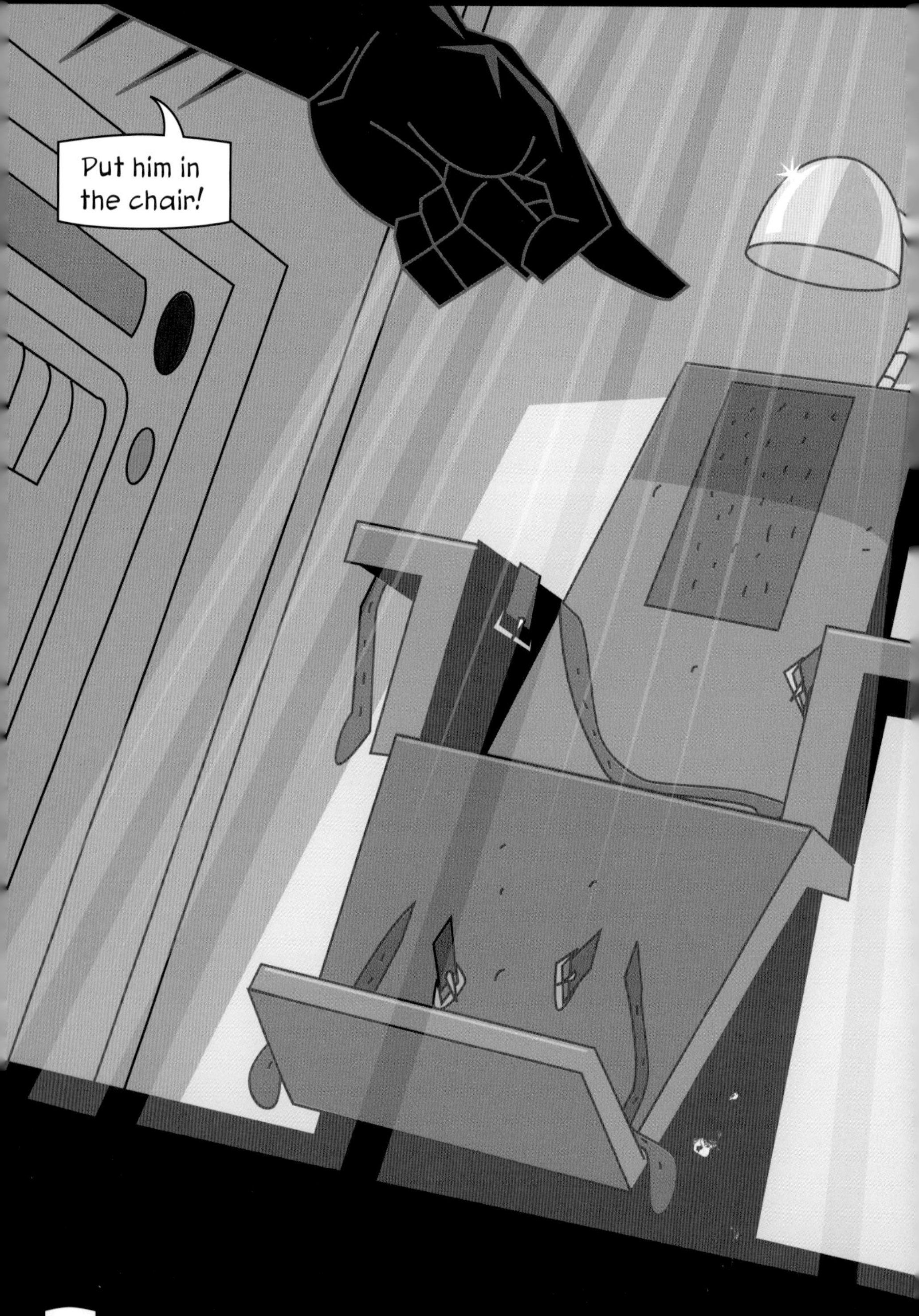
Put him in the chair!

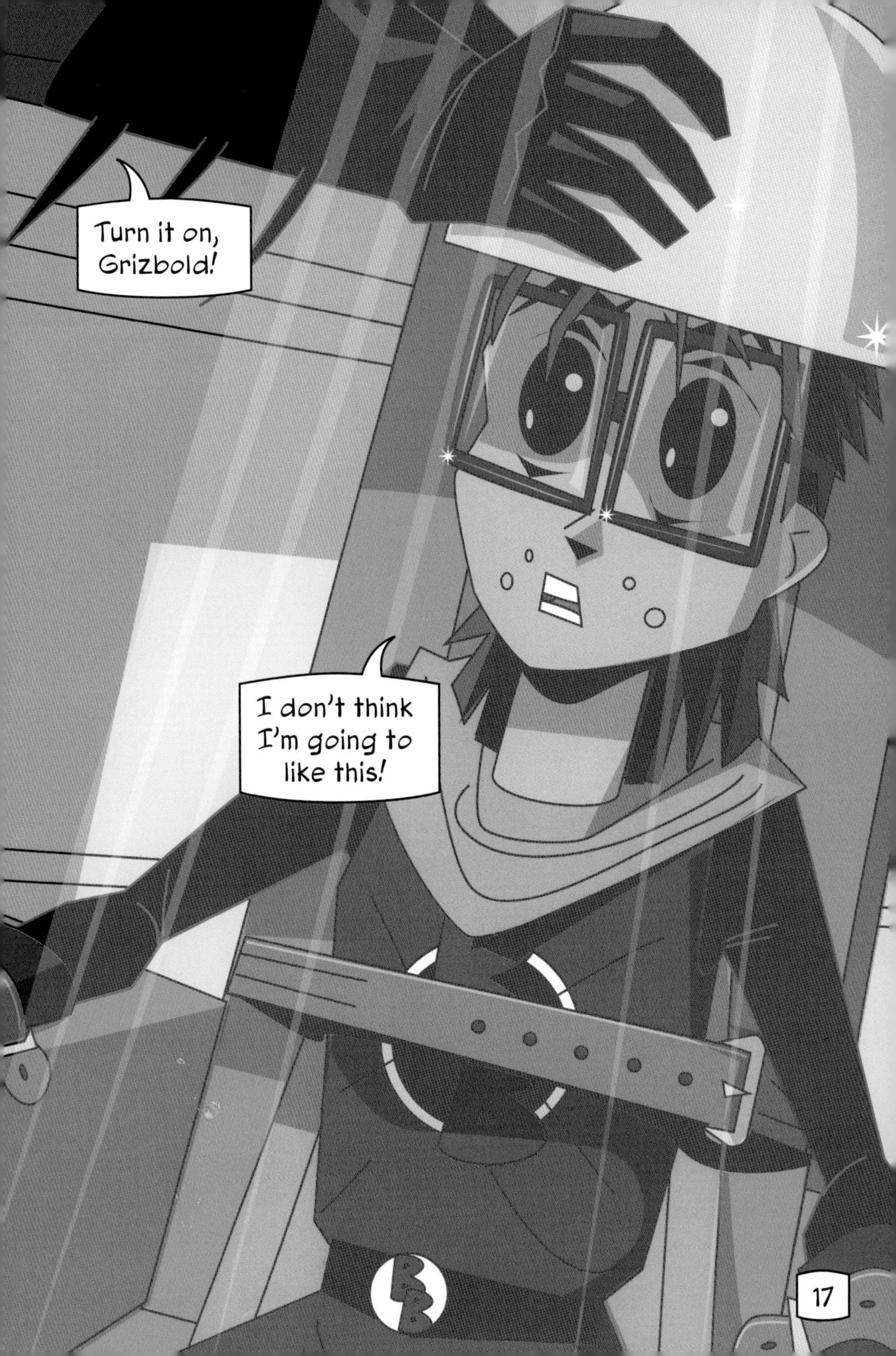
Turn it on, Grizbold!
I don't think I'm going to like this!

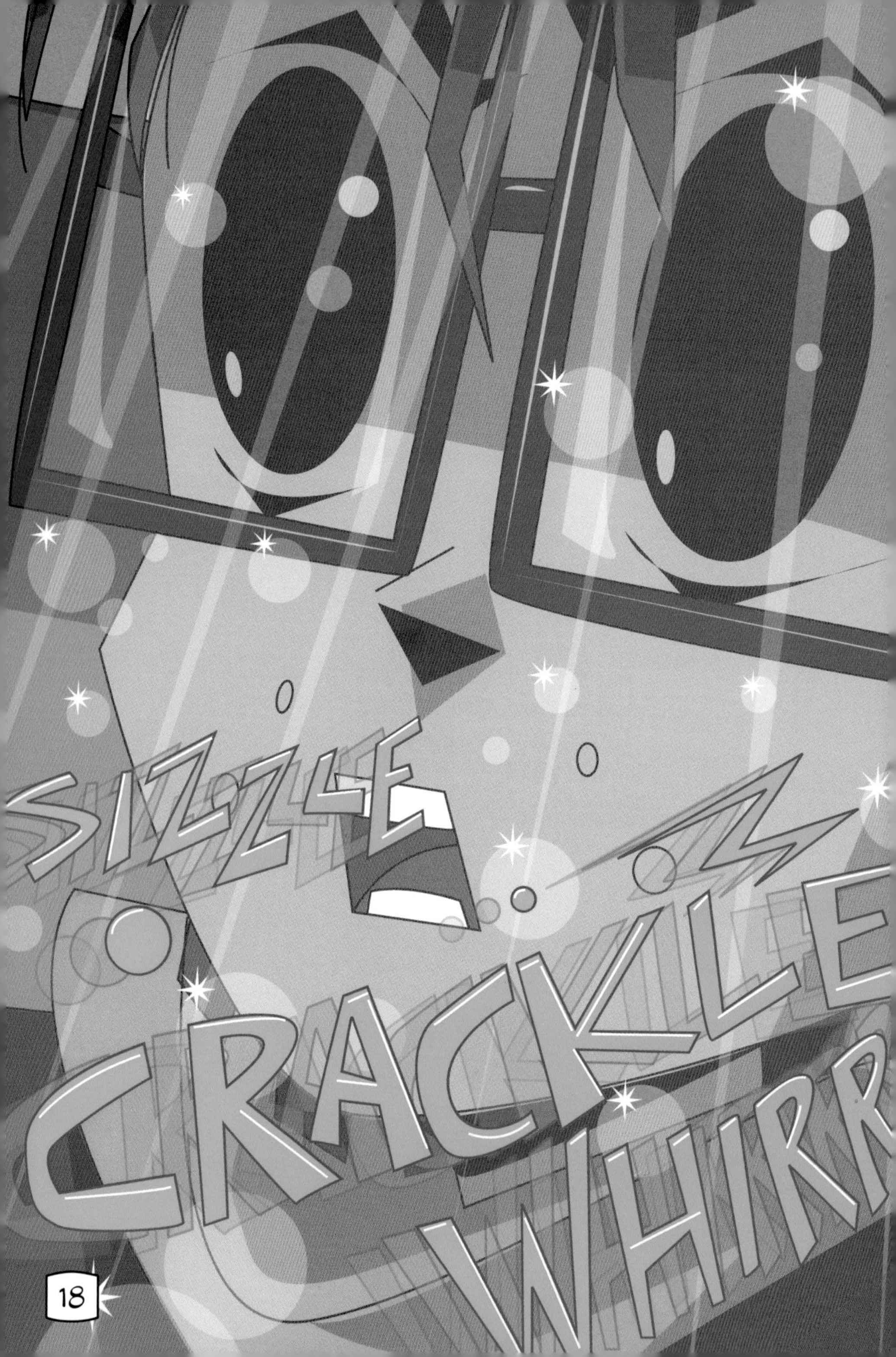
SIZZLE
CRACKLE
WHIRR

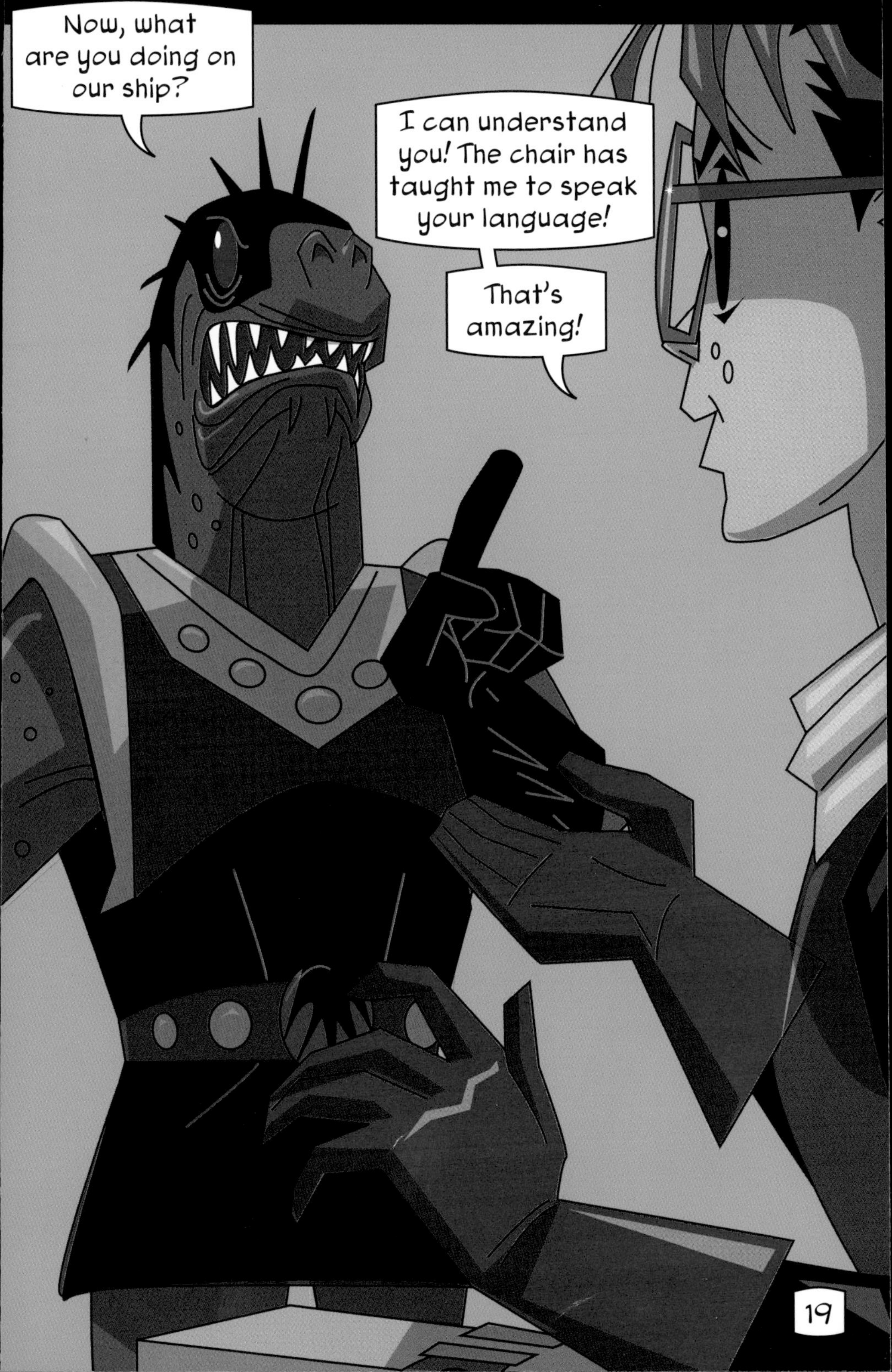

Now, what are you doing on our ship?
I can understand you! The chair has taught me to speak your language!
That's amazing!

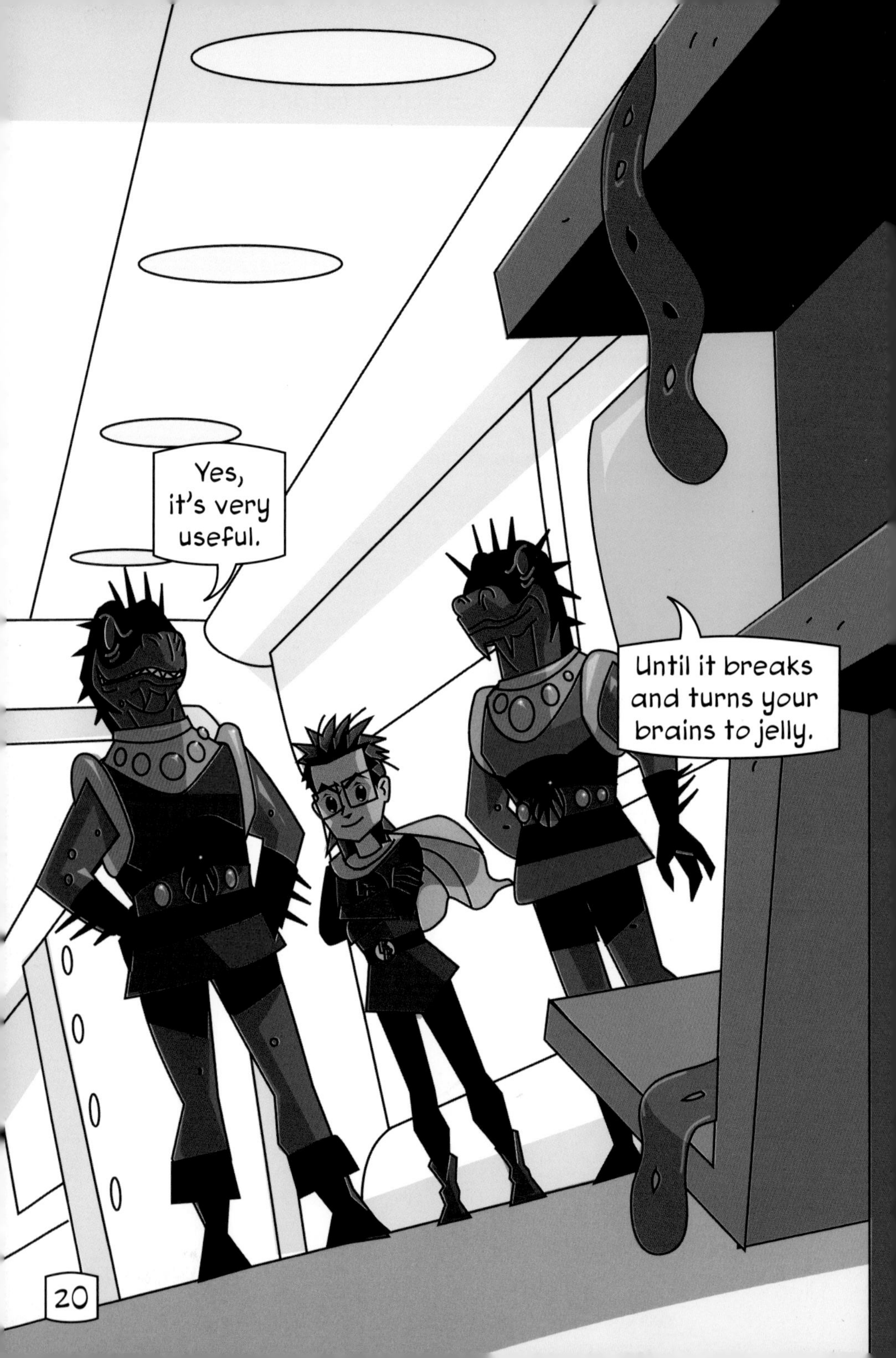
Yes, it's very useful.
Until it breaks and turns your brains to jelly.

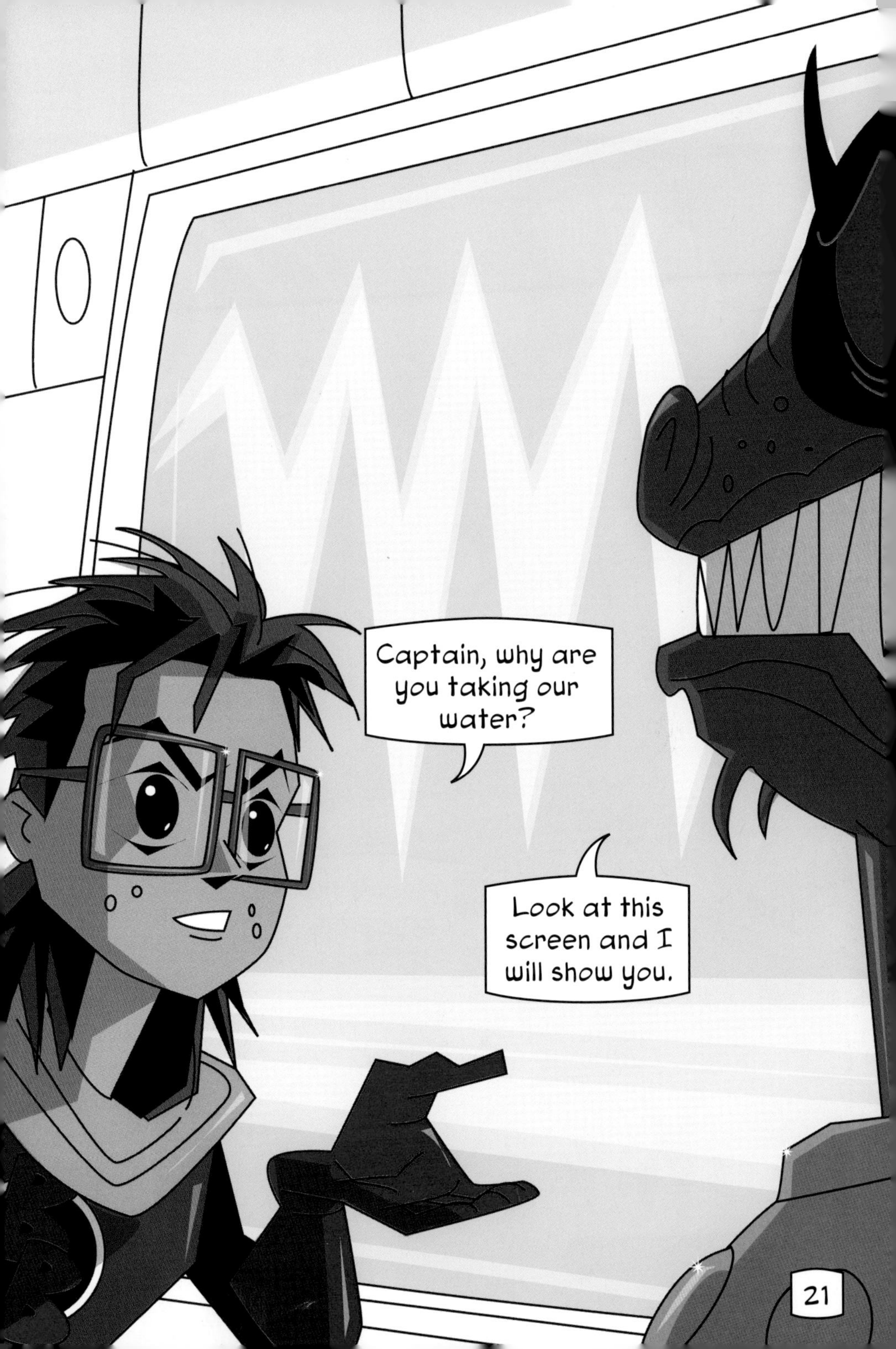
Captain, why are you taking our water?
Look at this screen and I will show you.

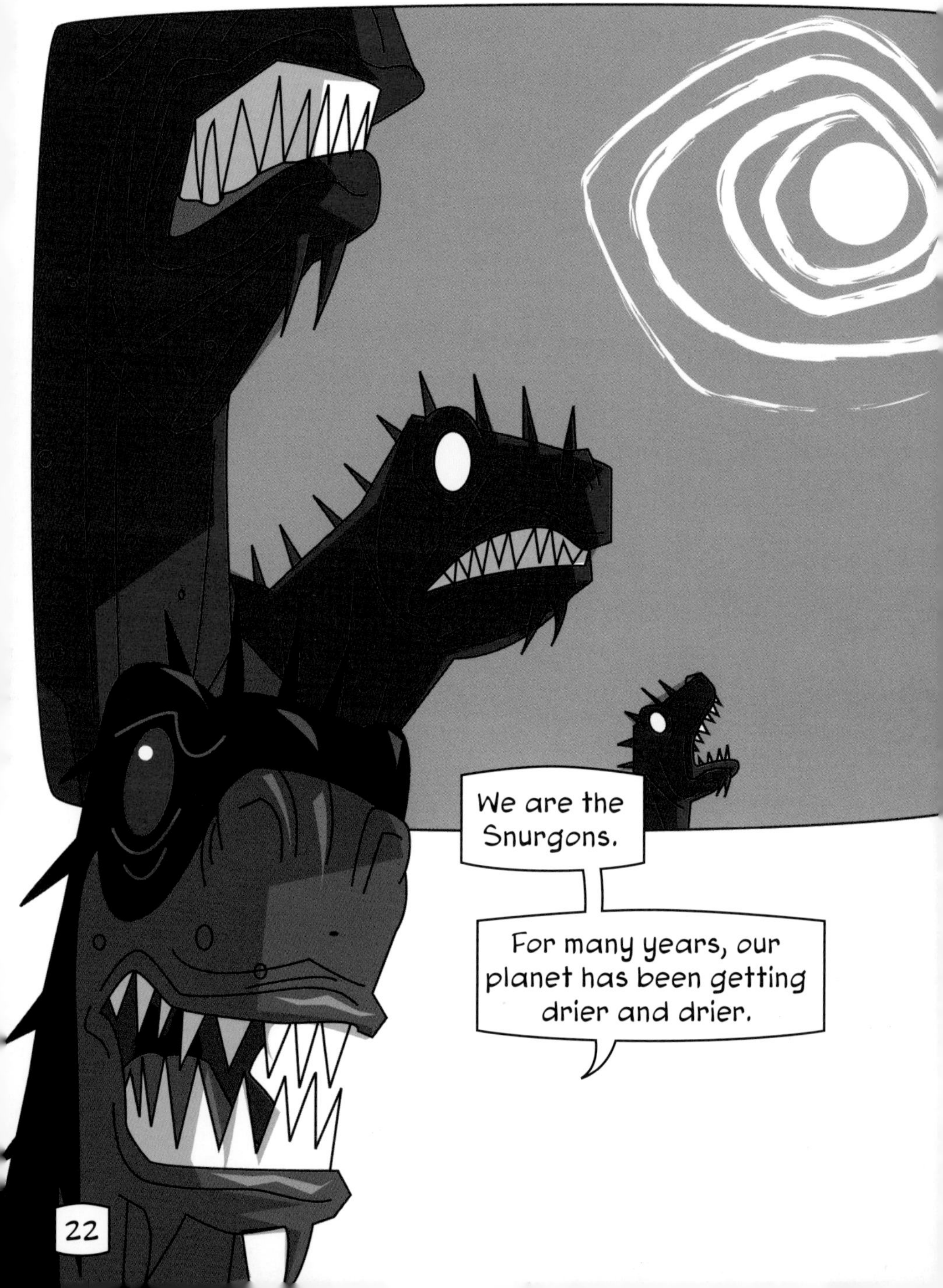
We are the Snurgons.
For many years, our planet has been getting drier and drier.

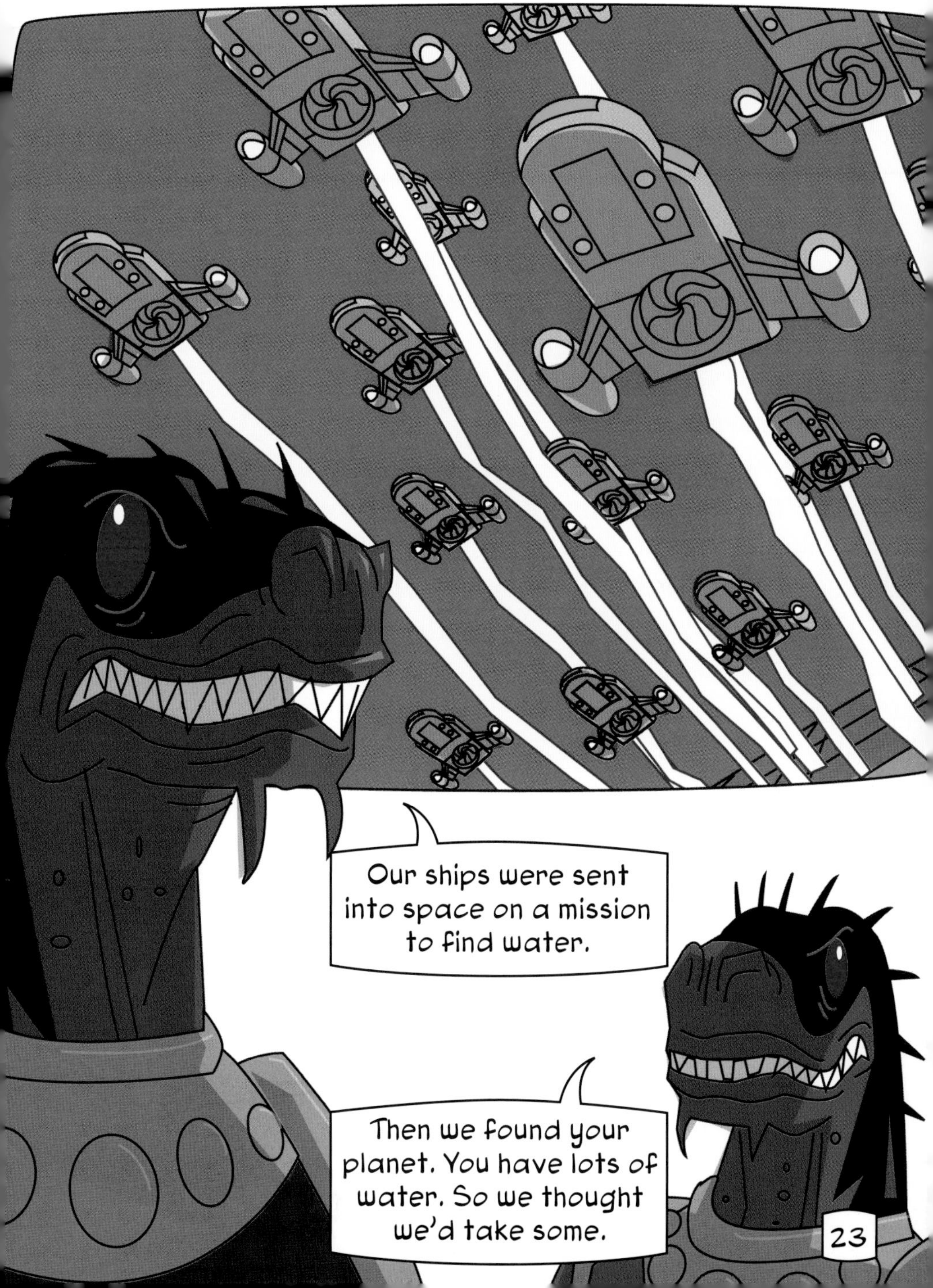
Our ships were sent into space on a mission to find water.
Then we found your planet. You have lots of water. So we thought we'd take some.

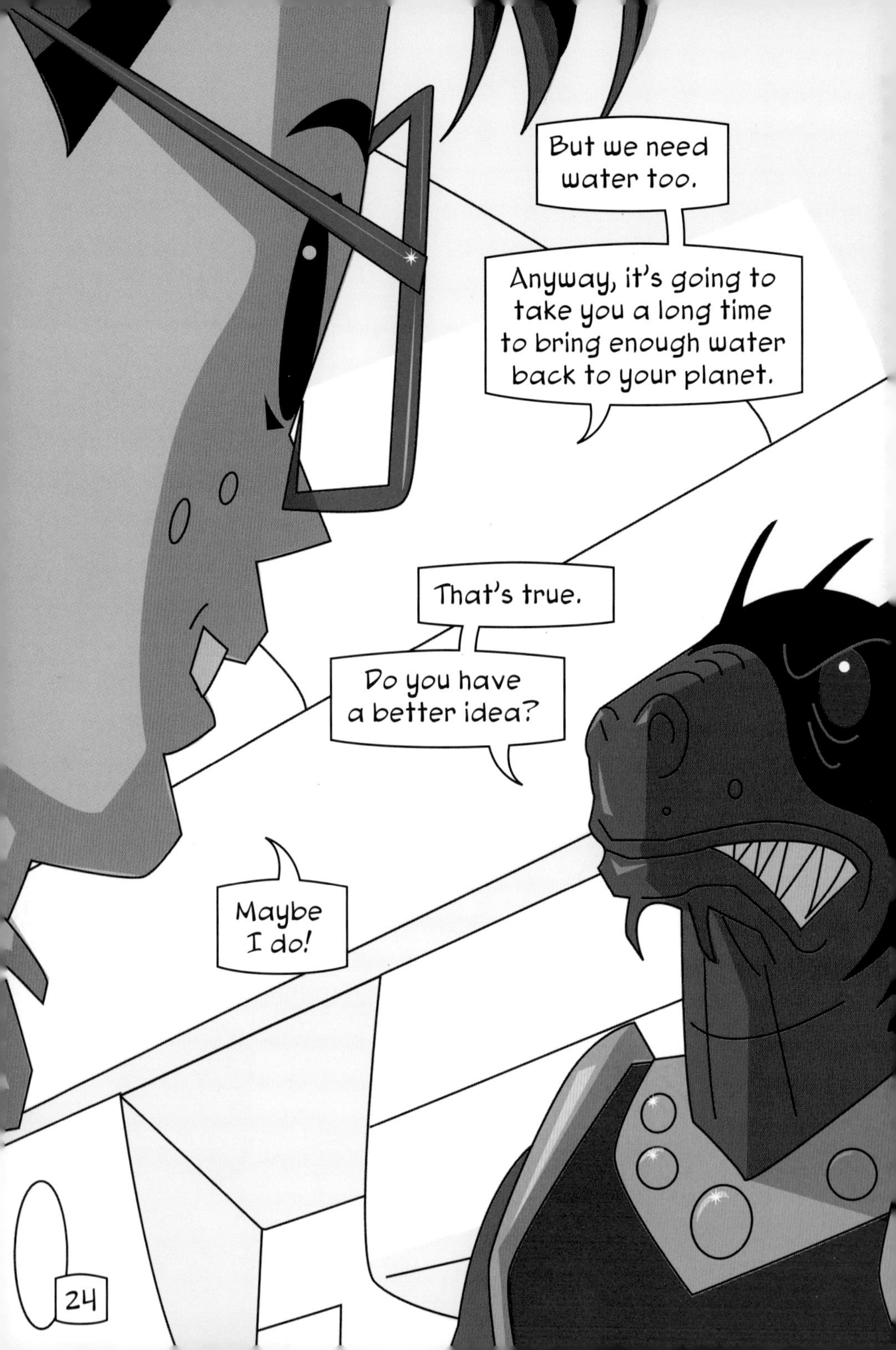
But we need water too.
Anyway, it's going to take you a long time to bring enough water back to your planet.
That's true.
Do you have a better idea?
Maybe I do!

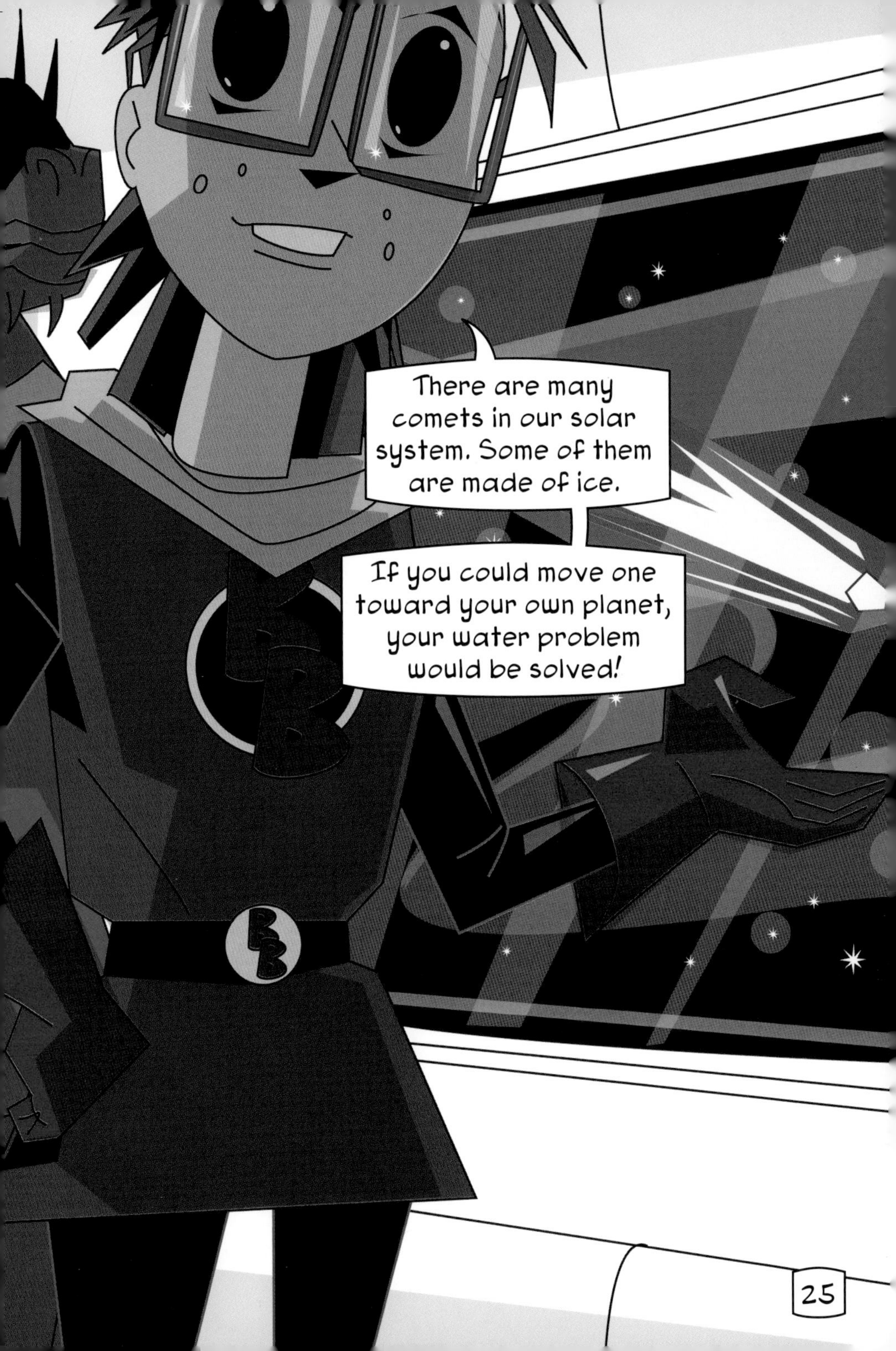
There are many comets in our solar system. Some of them are made of ice.
If you could move one toward your own planet, your water problem would be solved!

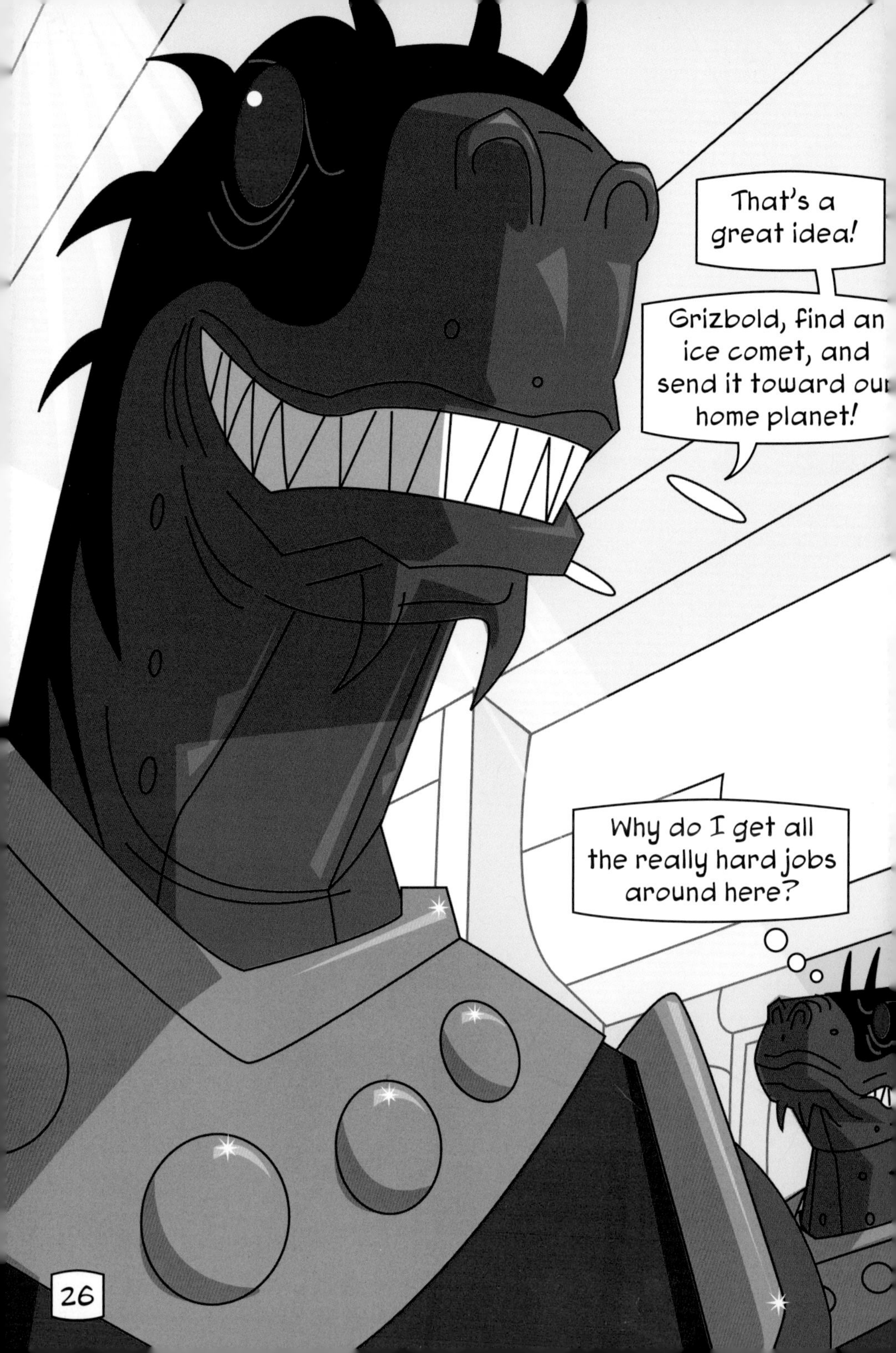
That's a great idea!
Grizbold, find an ice comet, and send it toward our home planet!
Why do I get all the really hard jobs around here?

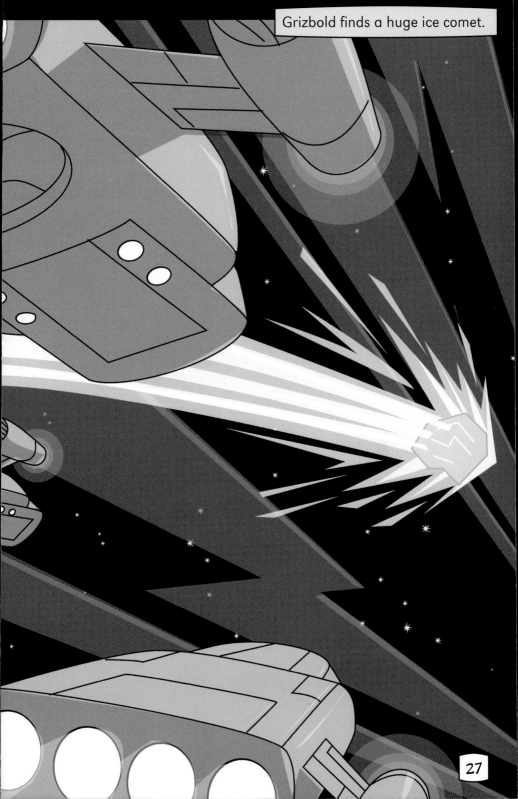

Grizbold finds a huge ice comet.

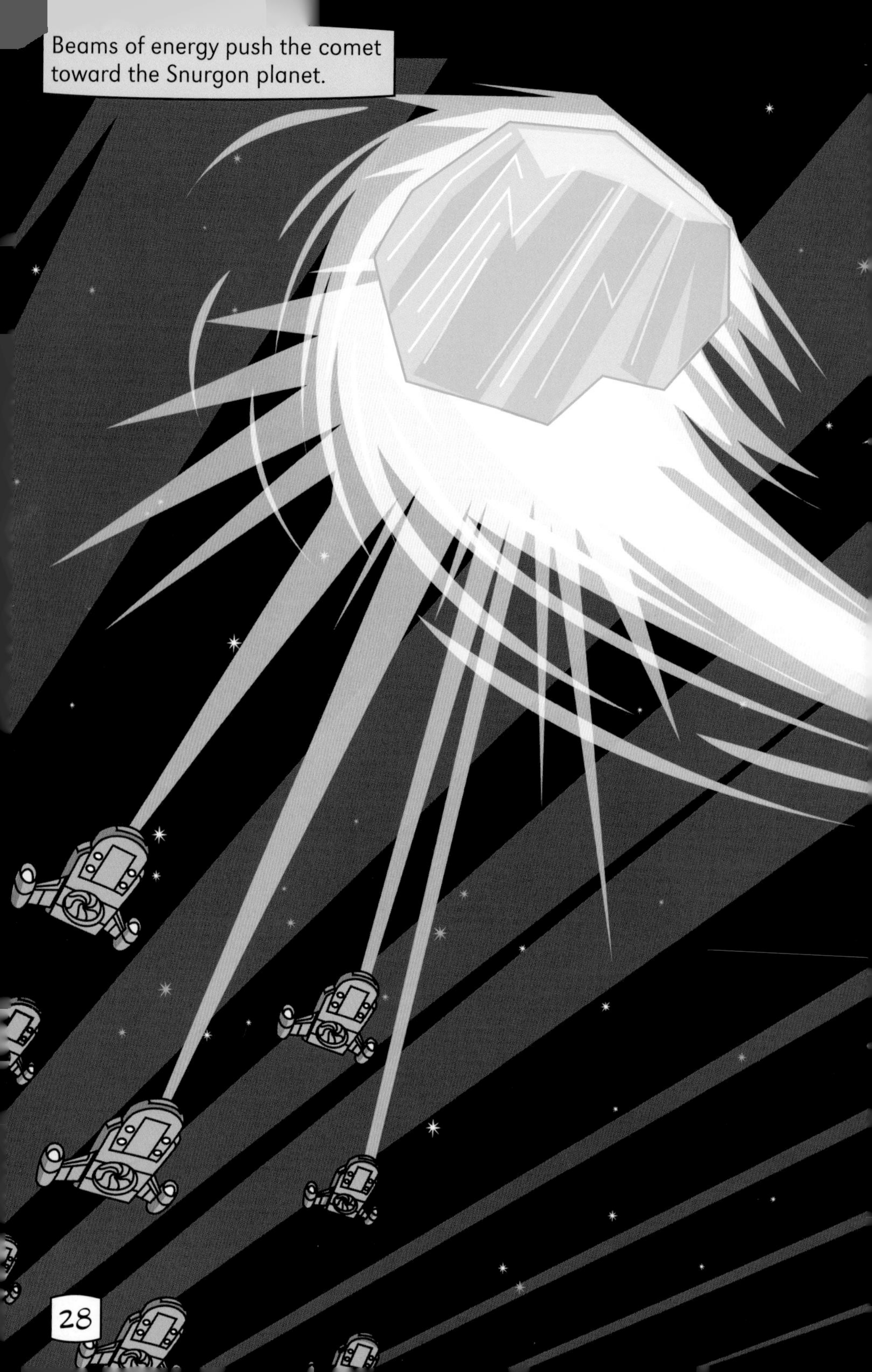
Beams of energy push the comet
toward the Snurgon planet.

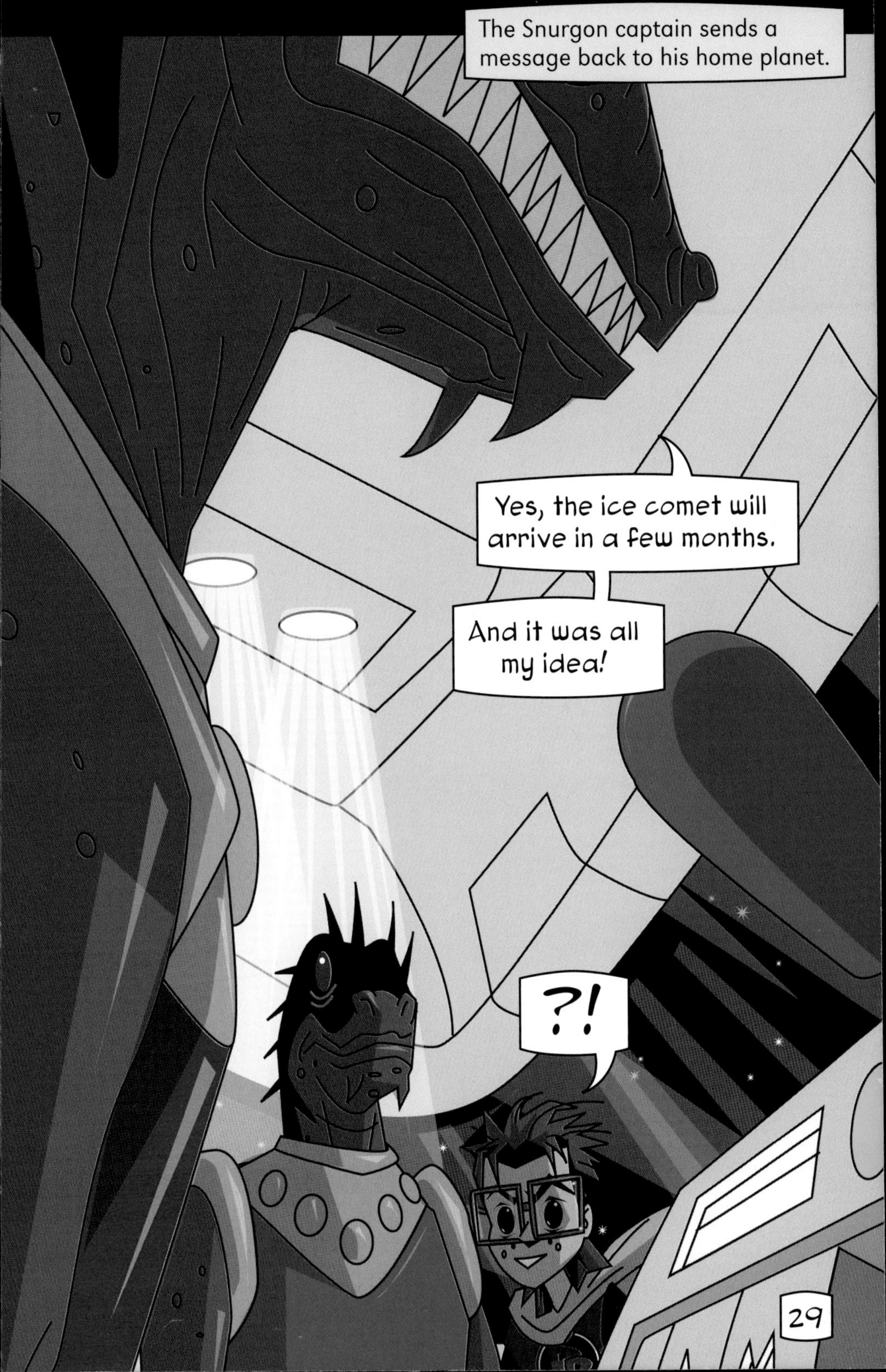
The Snurgon captain sends a message back to his home planet.
Yes, the ice comet will arrive in a few months.
And it was all my idea!
?!

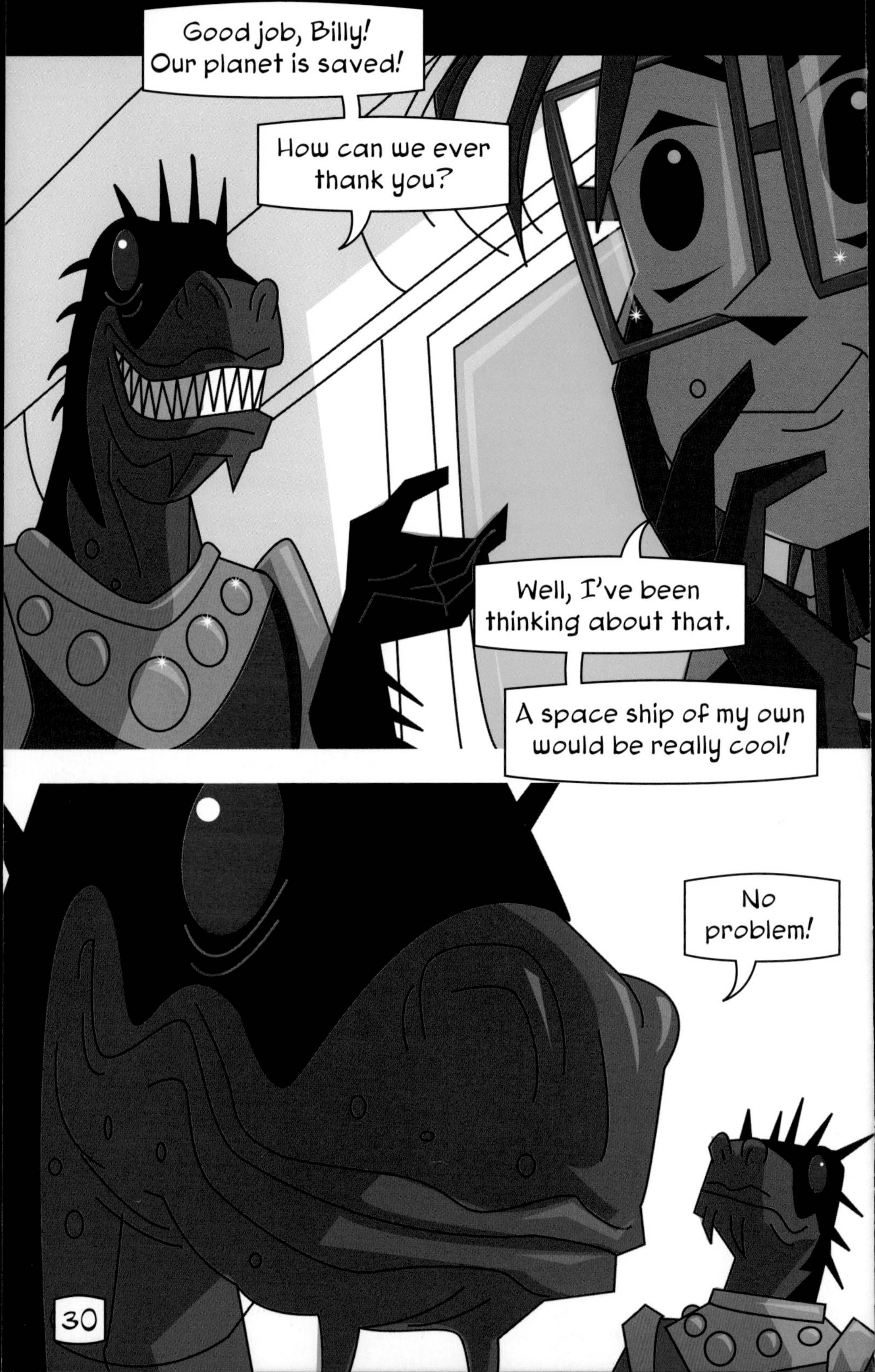
Good job, Billy! Our planet is saved!
How can we ever thank you?
Well, I've been thinking about that.
A space ship of my own would be really cool!
No problem!

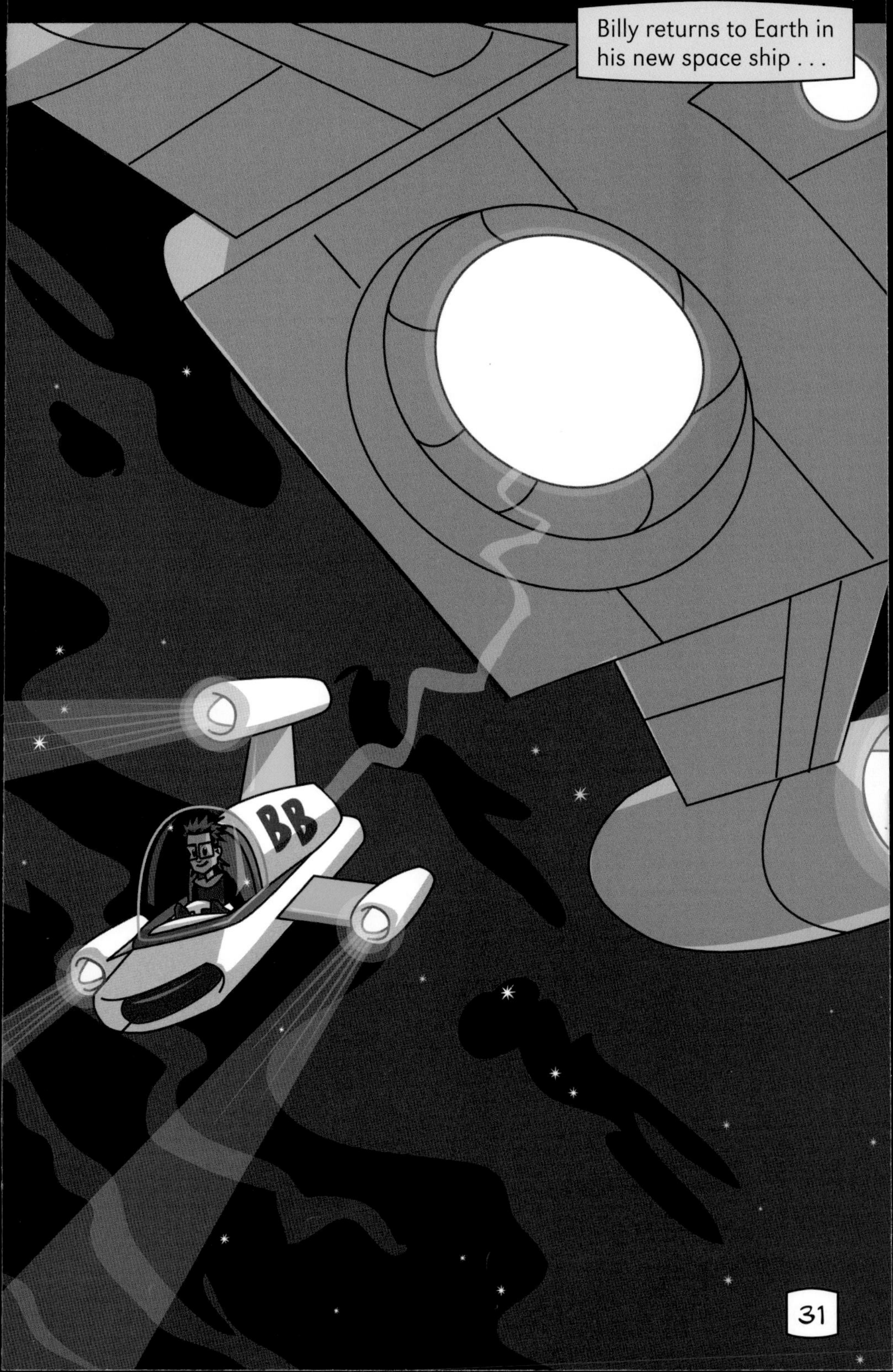
Billy returns to Earth in his new space ship . . .
BB

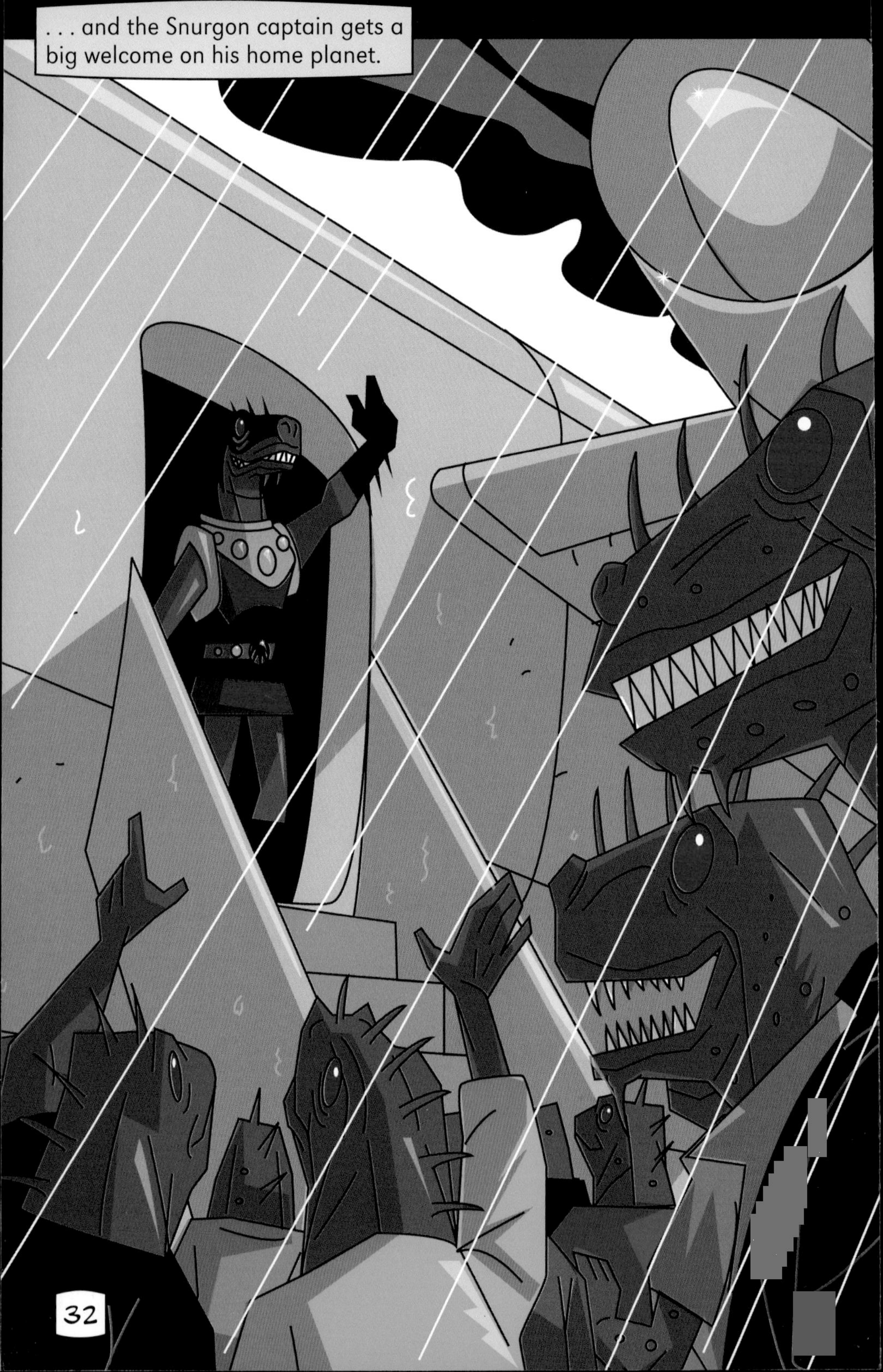
. . . and the Snurgon captain gets a big welcome on his home planet.

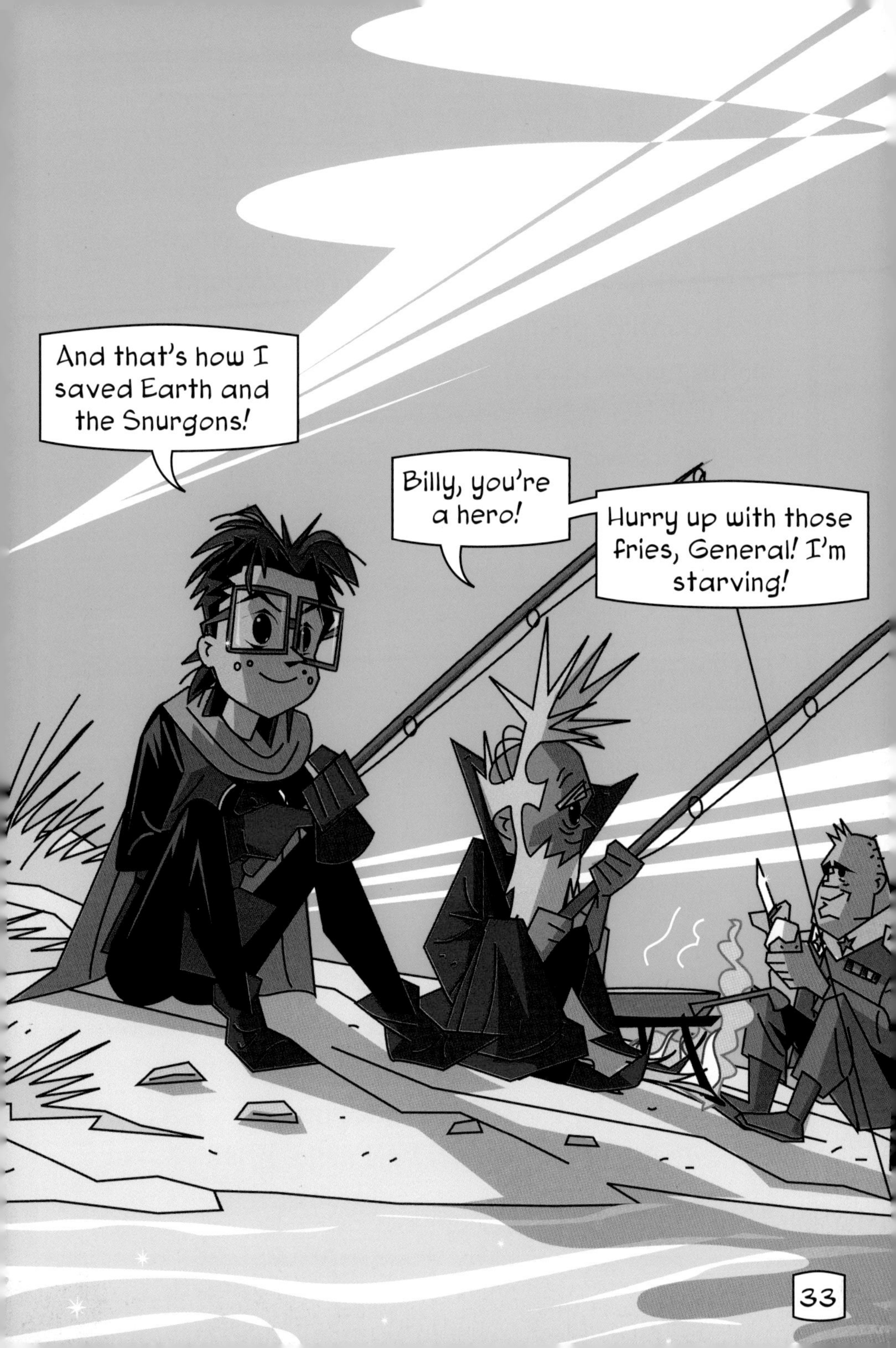
And that's how I saved Earth and the Snurgons!
Billy, you're a hero!
Hurry up with those fries, General! I'm starving!

ABOUT THE AUTHOR

David Orme was a teacher for 18 years before he became a full-time writer. When he is not writing books, he travels around the country, giving performances, running writing workshops, and running courses. David has written more than 250 books, including poetry collections and anthologies, fiction and nonfiction, and school textbooks. He currently lives in Winchester, England.

ABOUT THE ILLUSTRATOR

Peter Richardson's illustrations have appeared in a variety of productions and publications. He has done character designs and storyboards for many of London's top animation studios as well as artwork for advertising campaigns by big companies like BP and British Airways. His work often appears in *The Sunday Times* and *The Guardian*, as well as many magazines. He loves the Billy Blaster books and looks forward to seeing where Billy and his ninja sidekick, Wu Hoo, will end up next.

GLOSSARY

alien (AY-lee-uhn)—a creature from another planet

beams (BEEMZ)—rays or bands of light

comet (KOM-it)—a bright object in space with a long tail made of gas and dust

dangerous (DAYN-jur-uhss)—likely to cause harm or injury

energy (EN-ur-jee)—power that makes machines work. Energy produces heat.

mission (MISH-uhn)—a special job or task

restaurant (RESS-tuh-rahnt)—a place where people pay to eat food

Snurgons (SNUR-gonz)—lizard-like aliens from a faraway desert planet

solar system (SOH-lur SISS-tuhm)—the sun and the planets that move in orbit around it

starving (STARV-ing)—suffering from a lack of food

submarine (suhb-muh-REEN)—a ship that can travel under the water

WHY IS WATER IMPORTANT?

The Snurgons traveled across space to bring water to their home planet. That's a long trip just to get some water! They went to the right place. Earth has lots of water.

Earth's surface is about 75 percent water. However, only a very small amount of the Earth's water is drinkable. Drinkable water is found in rivers, freshwater lakes, or underground.

Earth's oceans hold about 97 percent of the Earth's water. We can't drink the water from the oceans because there is too much salt in it. However, scientists are working on ways to make the ocean water drinkable.

The human body is mostly water. Water makes up almost 70 percent of an adult's body. A newborn baby's body is made up of even more water — almost 80 percent!

The average person needs to drink half a gallon of water or more per day. While it is possible for a person to go without food for more than a month, you wouldn't live for more than a few days without water.

If you don't drink enough water per day, you will become dehydrated (dee-HYE-dray-tid). Dehydration is dangerous. If you are dehydrated, you might feel thirsty or very tired. It's a good idea to drink several glasses of water every day to prevent dehydration.

If you don't drink enough water, your body can't fight off diseases very well. No wonder water is so important to the Snurgons. Nobody wants to get sick!

DISCUSSION QUESTIONS

1. The Snurgons are aliens from another planet. Do you think aliens exist? If so, what do you think they look like? Do you think aliens have visited Earth before?

2. Most of the Earth is covered with water. The Snurgons come from a planet that has almost no water. How would it be different on Earth if the oceans were deserts instead? What would life on Earth be like?

3. The Snurgons are more friendly to Billy after he helps them. Why? Do you think Billy did the right thing by helping the Snurgons?

WRITING PROMPTS

1. Billy Blaster is a super hero. He uses his brains and tools to help Earth. Pretend you're a super hero. What are your super powers? Do you fight crime? Solve mysteries? Save aliens? Write about your adventures!

2. The Snurgons put Billy in a chair. The chair teaches Billy how to talk to the Snurgons. If you could talk to aliens, what would you say? What kinds of questions would you ask them?

3. The Snurgon captain gives Billy a brand new ship. If you had your own space ship, what would it look like? What planets would you visit? Who would you take with you?

INTERNET SITES

Do you want to know more about subjects related to this book? Or are you interested in learning about other topics? Then check out FactHound, a fun, easy way to find Internet sites.

Our investigative staff has already sniffed out great sites for you!

Here's how to use FactHound:

1. Visit *www.facthound.com*

2. Select your grade level.

3. To learn more about subjects related to this book, type in the book's ISBN number: 9781434212672.

4. Click the Fetch It button.

FactHound will fetch the best Internet sites for you!